Benjamin Leopold Farjeon

The March ofFate

A Novel: Vol.III.

Benjamin Leopold Farjeon

The March ofFate
A Novel: Vol.III.

ISBN/EAN: 9783337031855

Printed in Europe, USA, Canada, Australia, Japan

Cover: Foto ©Andreas Hilbeck / pixelio.de

More available books at **www.hansebooks.com**

THE MARCH OF FATE.

A Novel.

BY

B. L. FARJEON,

AUTHOR OF

"GREAT PORTER SQUARE," "TOILERS OF BABYLON,"
"A YOUNG GIRL'S LIFE," "THE MYSTERY OF M. FELIX," &c.

IN THREE VOLUMES.

VOL. III.

LONDON :
F. V. WHITE & CO.,
31, SOUTHAMPTON STREET, STRAND, W.C.
1893.

CONTENTS.

The Fourth Link—Retribution.

THE MARCH OF FATE.

THE MARCH OF FATE.

The Fourth Link—Retribution.

CHAPTER XXIX.

THE PALACE OF PLEASURE.

IT was the night before the Derby, and the Royal Palace of Pleasure was crowded. Every portion of the palatial building, with one exception, was packed by an audience drawn from all classes of society, St. James and St. Giles and all their various intermediate grades being fully represented. To these mixed qualities, from the highly intelligent to the idiotically vacuous, the entertainment provided by the enterprising managers of the Royal Palace of Pleasure appeared to be equally palatable. Even the thoughtful-minded sat, and looked, and listened with apparent satisfaction.

The one unoccupied portion of the music hall was a capacious stage box on the O. P. side, which ·the habitual humble frequenters of the Palace of Pleasure regarded with some such feelings as they would have regarded the Throne Room of a real Royal palace. That it was engaged and was intended to be occupied some time during the evening was evident from the preparations which had been made for expected visitors. Costly bouquets had been provided, and special programmes printed on satin; and it was observed by the aforesaid habitual frequenters that new chairs with gilt backs had been put into the box. Communicating with this box at the back were two private apartments, completely hidden from the view of the audience, one a dressing-room for ladies, the other a saloon luxuriously furnished. At the present moment it was more than usually attractive with a display of glass, and fruit, and flowers; and a promise of revelry was held out by two ice pails containing some dozen bottles of '74 Pommery.

"I ,say Bill," whispered a woman to her neighbour in the gallery, " who's a-coming to-night 'in that box there? Some swells, I should say, by the looks of it."

"I did 'ear," replied Bill, who was generally supposed to be gifted with witty and sarcastic power, " that 'er between-July-and-September Majesty the Queen is going to honour us with a visit, for the special purpose of 'earing wot's going to win the Derby. She's got a dollar or two she wants to put on."

" Git out with yer," said the woman. " Wot d'yer mean with yer between-July-and-September Majesty? "

"Don't yer know?" exclaimed Bill. " You've been nicely brought up, you 'ave. Wot month comes between July and September? "

" August, o' course."

" That's it," said Bill, chuckling. " That's wot they call the Queen—her August Majesty."

" Wot do they call 'er that for? "

31*

"There yer floor me," said Bill. "Blest if I know. The next time she comes to see me I'll arks 'er."

"Wot's going to win the Derby, Bill?" asked the woman coaxingly.

"D'yer think I'm going to tell yer for nothink?" retorted Bill. "Not me."

"I'll stand yer a pint, Bill, if yer give me the tip."

"All right, old gal. The favourite's going to win, as sure as yer've got a 'ead on yer shoulders. I ain't going to break my jaw in pernouncing 'is name. It commences with A, and ends with A, and it's got a lot of A's in the middle. There's the straight tip for yer, and don't yer forgit it."

"Ain't Morning Glory got a chance, Bill?"

"Morning Glory!" exclaimed Bill, with intense feeling. "Not a ghost of a chance. I got it from 'Arry Lobb—he's in the training stable, yer know. Well, he ses, ses 'Arry, that the favorite's on the job this time, and nothink can stop 'im. I wouldn't tell it to everybody, but I'll tell it to you, 'cause you ain't 'arf a bad sort—put your bottom dollar on the favourite, and yer'll see 'im romp in. I got four to one a month ago, and now it's a even chance. My brother the Lurcher ses he to me, he ses, 'If I wos you, Bill, I'd 'edge.' 'Edge! Not if I know it. It ain't orfen yer git a certainty, and this is too good a thing to throw away. Wot do *you* think?" The speaker suddenly paused, and with two curled palms of his hands before his eyes made as if he was looking through a pair of opera glasses. "Well, I'm blest! D'yer see that bloke there in the box, looking at the flowers?"

"Yes, I see 'im, Bill."

"That's Mr. Redwood, as the favourite belongs to. I'll bet that's 'is private box, and that he's got a party coming to night. He used to race in the name of Larkworthy, but he sails in 'is own boat now. All through a woman, I've 'eerd, as he's nuts on."

"Who's the woman, Bill?"

"You know 'er. Everybody knows 'er. 'Onoria. She's a lucky one, she is—and what a beauty! You'd like to stand in 'er shoes, you would."

"Not my luck! D'yer think it's 'er that's coming to the box to-night?"

"It's odds on, I should say."

"I am glad, that I am. I've never set eyes on 'er. I'd sooner see 'er than the Queen, that I would."

"You'll see something when she sets in the box there with 'er back to the stage. She always does that; it's one of 'er tricks, and she's as full of 'em as an unbroken colt. Yes, you'll see something worth seeing. She's a blaze of dymens, she is; the Princess of Wales don't dress 'arf as well."

"And that Mr. Redwood there is sweet on 'er. I can't say I like the looks of 'im."

"You'd put up with 'im if he took a fancy to yer. Sweet on 'er! That's not 'arf wot he is. He's mad in love with 'er, and they do say she treats 'im as if he was no better than the dirt under 'er feet.

"Ah," said the woman proudly, "she knows 'er way about, she does. Good luck to 'er! The minute a woman gives way to a man he's ready to set 'is 'eel on 'er. I've found that out, and if my time was to come over 'agin them as made up to me would see the difference. I suppose Mr. Redwood gives 'er the dymens she wears."

"He fairly loads 'er with 'em. My brother the Lurcher knows the sister of a servant of 'er'n, and she tells 'im a lot. She's a rum 'un is 'Onoria in more ways than one. Sometimes when Mr. Redwood comes to see 'er she calls out 'erself, 'Tell Mr. Redwood I'm not at 'ome.' That's cool, ain't it?"

"It's the way to serve 'em. He must be very rich to give 'er all them presents."

"There's no end to 'is money, and he's going the pace, he is. 'Ere's Baby Biffin. That's yer style!"

A performance on the trapeze had permitted of this conversation without disturbing the enjoyment of the audience, but the appearance of Baby Biffin on the stage put an end to it. Baby Biffin was not a baby; she was a woman grown, of goodly proportions,

and her age could not have been less than
twenty-five. Nevertheless, she dressed (or,
rather undressed), posed, and conducted herself as a child of tender years, under most
extraordinary and unnatural conditions, might
by a miracle have done. The presumption is
a daring one, and is made here merely
because a large majority of the audience
derived enjoyment from her performance,
and saw nothing discrepant in it. She rolled
her eyes, she minced and lisped her words,
she pouted, she twisted her body, she sang in
a fashion by no means infantile. A more
complete parody upon the title she had
assumed and was known by in music hall
circles could scarcely be conceived. In the
display of her person she left little to the
imagination, her actions were vulgar and
coarse, her voice was brassy, her features
were thick with paint, her hair (there were
several heads of it) hung below her waist.
There were rumours of her having entangled
a young gentleman of noble lineage, and
this was regarded as a distinction, and un-

doubtedly added to her popularity. During
her singing and dancing she carried on a
running interlude with vacuous swells in stalls
and 'boxes, which fired them into immense
enthusiasm. They laughed, they crowed,
they clapped their hands, they wriggled their
shoulders, they went into convulsions of
delight, they threw flowers to her, they
shouted the refrain to her popular song, " I
am such a delicate duck, dear boys. Duck,
dear boys, Duck, dear boys," and when she
finally retired, throwing kisses to them from
the tips of her fingers, which were plastered
with rings, she was followed with deafening
applause. The most harmless and enjoyable
contributors to the entertainment in this
Royal Palace of Pleasure were those who per-
formed in dumb show—such as a slack rope
dancer, an illusionist, and a Japanese, whose
manipulation of knives, cups, balls, plates,
and other requirements of his art, was mar-
vellous. Of the others who sang and danced
at least half were vulgar and coarse, and some
indecent. It was not the words to which

objection could be taken—though they were,
as a rule, silly enough, and utterly devoid of
literary merit—but the actions which accompanied them, the suggestive leer or wink,
which conveyed into the words an interpre-
tation which should never be allowed in a
place of public entertainment.

On this night less attention than usual was
paid to the artists. In such places as the
Palace of Pleasure the night before the Derby
is a night of nights; to many it is the night
of the year. The excitement and animation
were wonderful; the prevailing dominant
thought was the race which was to be run
to-morrow. The name of the favourite, which
Bill in the gallery declined to pronounce, was
Abracadabra; the name of the second
favourite was Morning Glory. Would the
favourite win? That was the burning, the
almost vital, question of the hour. A wild
delirium raged through the house, from floor
to ceiling, from the back of the gallery to the
back of the stage. The fevered pulses beat
rhythmically : Would the—Favour—Ite win?

Would the—Favour—Ite win? Would the—
Favour—Ite win? Everyone answered the
question in the affirmative, and yet everyone
continued to ask it of his neighbour. There
was scarcely a person in all that vast multi-
tude who did not have some direct or indirect
interest in the race—a chance in a sweep, a
bet or a share in a bet, from thousands of
pounds down to a threepenny piece, and
every speaking or singing artist who appeared
upon the stage contrived to introduce the
subject in a manner agreeable to the audience.
In the next private box to that containing a
bevy of painted harridans sat a doctor, an
author, a soldier, and an editor, all of them
famous, and these were discussing Abracadabra. In the stalls were young and old
swells " seeing life," youthful members of the
aristocracy fresh from college, coming or
come into their fortunes, swindling hawks
who were tracking them down, a large
sprinkling of the demi-monde, lawyers, visitors
from the country, and other component parts
of fashion and society, and these were discuss-

ing Abracadabra.   In the pit were respectable
working men and their wives, young artisans
and their sweethearts a-courting, clerks, shop-
keepers, and others of the middle strata, and
these were discussing Abracadabra.   In the
gallery were shop-boys, work-girls, appren-
tices, costermongers, labourers, and the
sweepings of the streets and lodging-houses,
and these were discussing Abracadabra.   Behind the scenes and in the dressing-rooms, up
in the flies and down in the cellars, those
employed in the Royal Palace of Pleasure
were all discussing Abracadabra.   Sprinkled
over every portion of the house, before and
behind the footlights, were racing men of high
and low degree, owners, trainers, jockeys,
stable men and boys, touts, tipsters, bookmakers, and hangers-on, and these, though
they were in the swim, as the saying is, were
all discussing Abracadabra.   They were the
oracles of the night, and the words that
dropped from their lips were esteemed as
pearls of price, and were passed around with
profound admiration and respect.   When the

chances of other horses engaged in the great contest were spoken of, it was in a half-hearted, depreciatory fashion. Some said Morning Glory had a good chance; a few said there was a dark horse in the race that would open people's eyes; instances of hot favourites being beaten, anecdotes of Hermit at sixty-six to one, and of other noted winners, were freely circulated; but in the long run they all came back to Abracadabra, whose glory it was impossible to dim. "It's a moral;" "It's all over but the shouting;" "Have a bit on the favourite;" this was the sum of all the eager talk.

Naturally, when Mr. Louis Redwood was observed in the stage-box, attention was drawn to him by reason of his being Abra-cadabra's owner, and the whisper went round that he stood to lose a hundred thousand pounds upon his horse. Some said he looked anxious, some said it made no difference to him whether his horse won or not, that he had enough money to sink a ship, and so on, and so on. Opera glasses were levelled at him as he stood in the box, gazing insolently upon the sea of faces.

"That man is a study," observed the doctor, in the private box; "you should make use of him." This to the author, who nodded, with his eyes fixed upon Mr. Redwood's face.

"He's an infernal scoundrel, I've heard," observed the soldier.

The editor said nothing; as he gazed he was thinking of men who once were high, and now were low.

A sound of voices and the rustling of skirts in the rear of the private box in which Louis Redwood was standing drew him away, and he went and opened the door.

"Honoria!" he cried, holding out his hands, with an eager light in his eyes. He was not acting a part; for once in his life the man was genuine and sincere.

"Ah, Redwood," said Honoria, in a careless tone. He offered to assist her in removing her wraps, but she said, "No, thank you," in her coldest voice, and turned

to a gentleman who had accompanied her
into the box, and accepted his assistance
instead.

"Good evening, Redwood," said this gentleman.

"Good evening, Major," said Redwood.

Major Causton was a middle-aged gentleman, with a long tawny moustache, which he
twisted and twirled when his hands were not
otherwise employed. Honoria glanced at the
two men and smiled.

"You are late, Honoria," said Redwood.

"Am I?" said Honoria, and stepped to the
front of the box. The stage was vacant at
this moment, and the superb beauty of the
notorious woman drew everybody's eyes upon
her.

"There's 'Onoria," said Bill in the gallery.

"Why, you said she'd be a blaze of dymens,"
cried the disappointed woman.

There was not a jewel upon Honoria. She
was dressed in black; straight, upright, and
regally beautiful, she stood in full view of the
house, perfectly unmoved and self-possessed.

A group of artists in a corner of the stalls scanned her admiringly.

"Cleopatra," said one.

"Zenobia," said the second.

"The Magdalen," said the third.

"Which do you think is the most interesting study?" asked the author of the editor.

"The story of Honoria," said the editor, "should prove, from the cradle to the grave, to be one of the most remarkable of the age."

"Don't talk of the grave," said the soldier, "in connection with that lovely creature." He turned red. There was a dangerous magnetism in Honoria, and her eyes were turned in his direction.

"Are you acquainted with her history?" asked the author.

"Something of it," replied the editor.

"I should much like to hear it."

"Later on I will relate what I know. In some respects it is singular, in others common enough; but it promises developments."

"One can never foretell," remarked the doctor, "how these women will end."

"As a rule," said the author, "they suddenly disappear, and, after a torpid period, emerge as elderly ballet girls."

"Or as lodging-house keepers," suggested the doctor.

"That will not be Honoria's fate," said the editor. "She will not degenerate into either a lodging-house keeper or an elderly ballet girl, living upon past glories. Have you seen her ride?"

"Yes, and she is a perfect horsewoman. You open up another possibility. She may become, for a time, the star of a circus."

"That requires early training, in which respect Honoria is deficient. She is really remarkably beautiful. Nor is it a spring beauty, which perishes with the season. If she is careful of herself, her summer and winter will be quite as attractive."

"You are all talking heresy," interposed the soldier, warmly. "I elect myself her champion. She is as good as she is beautiful." The others exchanged a significant smile, which did not escape the soldier's observation. "Where are diamonds found?" he asked.

"In the most unlikely places," replied the editor.

"Washed out of the mire," said the soldier.

"True—in the rough. But this one is polished. You have lived long out of England, and are ignorant of the A B C of certain phases of our civilized life. You will grow wiser by and by, and will think as we do."

"God forbid!" said the soldier, gazing earnestly upon Honoria.

CHAPTER XXX

"Do you like the box?" asked Louis Redwood, as Honoria seated herself.

"It is like other boxes," she answered with an air of indifference.

He bit his lip. "I had these programmes printed for you." He put one of the satin slips before her. "The flowers please you, I hope?"

"I prefer simple flowers," she said.

"I will think of that next time."

"I would not trouble myself."

"You know the pleasure it gives me to consult your tastes, to gratify your wishes."

"Does it? Major Causton, is that a man or a woman singing?" Her back was towards the stage, and she was surveying the audience.

"An old woman," replied the Major, "in

32*

short skirts, casting amorous glances on gilded youth."

"How ridiculous! Causton is very amusing." This observation was addressed to Redwood.

" Very," he said, with a scowl.

" Copy him. You could not do better."

" I will give you lessons, Redwood," said the Major, with a broad grin on his face.

" Thank you; I do not require them."

" You are mistaken," said Honoria, without glancing at him. " You require them badly. Does he not, Major."

" I'll not venture to say," replied the Major, good-humouredly. " I find it difficult enough to steer my own boat."

She laughed aloud, and played with her fan.

" Honoria," said Redwood, in an undertone, bending over her, " I will do anything to please you."

" It does not look like it. Pray move away; I don't wish you to come so close to me."

" You are wearing me out," he muttered.

"Give it up, then," she retorted scornfully.

"I am not to be shaken off so easily," he said. "We shall see who will win in the end."·

"Yes, we shall. There is, after all, a little enjoyment in a battle of this kind." He took out his cigar case. "If you begin to smoke I shall leave the box." He replaced the case with a savage look. "What is the stable news?"

"Everything is right. The horse was never better in his life."

"You will win?"

"I can't lose."

"Don't reckon your chickens, Redwood." There was no malice in her tone; they were conversing now amicably.

"I reckon these. There never was such a certainty. I've been offered twenty thousand for my book."

"Lucky dog!" said Major Causton. "You win at everything."

"Not at everything," said Honoria. "Eh, Redwood?"

" Don't begin again, or I'll scratch the horse at the last minute."

" You would never dare to show your face on a race-course again if you did," said Honoria. " But if Abracadabra were out of the race what difference would that make to me ? "

" I'll tell you what you stand to win on him, if you like."

" Yes, do." From her words it might be supposed that she took an interest in the subject, but her voice betrayed the most absolute indifference.

Louis Redwood consulted his betting-book. " Twenty-eight thousand pounds," he said.

" And to lose ? "

" Nothing. You know that well enough."

" Causton," said Honoria, " how much do I stand to win on ' Morning Glory ' ? "

" What ! " cried Louis Redwood, white with rage.

" A true bill," she said calmly, " I've learnt something of the world, and I play my own game. How much, Major ? "

"Thirty odd thou., my dear."

"Stop that, if you please. Not even from you; not even to vex Redwood."

"I throw myself at your feet, lady fair," said Major Causton, undisturbed by the check, "but if you will be so infernally bewitching, what can a poor beggar do?"

"Do you mean to say," exclaimed Redwood, "that you've been backing 'Morning Glory' without my knowledge?"

"There's no denying it, is there, Major?"

"There's no denying it, lady fair."

"The Major," said Honoria, "has been my commission agent."

"For how long has this been going on?" asked Redwood.

"Ever since you began to put me on Abracadabra."

"You must be out of your senses."

"Very much in them, dear boy," said the Major. "Very much in them. Lady fair has brains. Brains! Hanged if the word expresses it. Her intellect is gigantic.

There's no stopping her, dear boy. But I'm telling tales out of school."

"I have no objection to Redwood's knowing everything now," said Honoria, smiling on the two men—a smile which caused the soldier in another private box to mutter under his breath, "By heavens, she's bewitching!" Honoria continued: "Make him acquainted with our proceedings, Major."

"Most interesting proceedings. Commenced in February."

"'Morning Glory' was at twenties then," volunteered Redwood.

"And twenty-fives, dear boy. Lady fair heard a whisper. A little bird came down the chimney, she said. A pretty fancy."

"One of those childish fancies," said Honoria, with composure, gazing steadily at Redwood, "that the children of the poor have. Did you know, Major, that I was once a very poor little girl, and sometimes had hardly enough to eat?"

"You don't say so, lady fair? It is

amazing. But what a romance! You're joking, though."

"I assure you I am not. Even up to the time I was eighteen I did not know what it was to have a sovereign in my purse. I was a very unfortunate young woman."

"You distress me, upon my honour you distress me. What an infernal hardship!"

"A very unfortunate, simple young woman," proceeded Honoria, very calmly; "I believed everything that was whispered into my silly little ears. I believed in truth, in honour, in faithfulness—I believed even in love."

"More and more like a romance. And did your lover deceive you? Show me the man. I will make an example of him."

"No; the subject annoys Redwood. He would rather hear about that little bird."

"It came down the chimney, she said, Redwood, and whispered, 'Morning Glory, Morning Glory.' She swore me to secrecy, and I put five hundred on for her at twenties and twenty-fives. She made other investments afterwards, when she won on the Lincoln, and a bit more two days afterwards, when she won on the Grand National."

" When ' Abracadabra's ' number goes up," said Redwood, " with ' Morning Glory ' fifth or sixth—that's about where he'll be—it will make a hole in your winnings. And serve you right."

" Mistaken, dear boy, mistaken," said Major Causton. " We've hedged, and stand to win either way. That is all I am permitted to disclose."

" You can tell him the other thing, Major."

" About ' Abracadabra,' lady fair ? "

" Yes."

" I am to hear now," said Redwood bitterly, " that you've been laying against my horse. I hope you have. Don't come to me to get you out of the mess."

" When do you think that is likely to occur ? " asked Honoria, with quiet scorn. " I am not accountable to you for my actions, and I advise you to be careful in the tone you adopt towards me."

"You're enough to drive a man mad," said Redwood. "Go on with your story, Causton, as I'm bound to hear it. More little birds, I suppose."

"You've fired straight this time, dear boy. Other little birds come down the chimney, and whisper to lady fair that Abracadabra will be second in the Derby."

"What wise little birds!" sneered Redwood. "But we've heard that sort of thing before. A woman lies in bed the night before a big race, with her window curtain up. Waking suddenly and opening her eyes she sees a star. The next day she relates her dream, and asks what star it was that shone upon her in the middle of the night, and is told it's Mars. That's the name of a horse in the race, and it happens that Mars wins. 'I knew it would,' she cries. 'What a fool I was not to back it! I shall never get such another chance.' It is easy to prophesy after the event. If by some cursed stroke of luck Abracadabra is second instead of first Honoria will be mourning that she didn't take advantage of the tip given to her by her little birds."

" She has taken advantage of it, dear boy. She has accepted fair odds that Abracadabra is second, and second only. She stands to win a pot on it."

"Indeed! I'll tell you what I'll do, Honoria. If Abracadabra is second in the Derby, I will make you a present of the horse."

" I hold you to your promise," said Honoria. " You are a witness, Major."

" I am, fair lady."

" Is a witness necessary?" asked Redwood, with suppressed passion. " Did you ever know me make a promise I didn't perform?"

"I do," said Honoria. " Carry your memory back, Redwood."

His face darkened; he knew to what she referred. They gazed at each other in silence for a few moments and then Honoria turned to the stage, upon which a fresh artist had just made his appearance.

He was the star of the evening, and the song
he was about to sing had been in everybody's
mouth, for weeks past. Men had reeled
through the street singing it tipsily, errand
boys had whistled it, policemen had hummed
it on their nightly beats, it had been accepted
as a charm, and its effect had been to considerably shorten the odds on the favourite for
the Derby. In point of literary merit it was
no better and no worse than the generality of
such effusions, but it had brought additional
popularity to the already popular singer, who
had sung it night after night in three different
music halls, the audiences in which had taken
up the refrain with that unanimous enthusiasm
which is a common feature in those places of
entertainment when a song strikes their fancy.
A single verse of the delectable stuff will
suffice for an illustration, one rhyme being
altered by the composer and singer in token
of its being trolled out the day before the
race was to be run :

" Stake your last dollar,
  Pawn your shirt collar—
Abracadabra
Is first past the post.
Beg, steal, or borrow,
Back me to-morrow,
Abracadabra
Has got 'em on toast.
Abracadabra,
Abracadabra,
Abracadabra
Has got 'em on toast."

The audience roared out the chorus at the top of their voices, and when the popular singer turned his back to them, and exhibited the letters of the horse's name so arranged perpendicularly and horizontally that Abracadabra was spelt either way, the laughter and applause became deafening. He was recalled half-a-dozen times, and each time sang a fresh encore verse which he had prepared for his admirers. At length he was allowed to retire for good, and the audience calmed down somewhat.

During this excitement Honoria had sat back in the box, in such a position that she could not be seen, and when comparative quiet reigned in the house, she asked Major Causton to call her carriage.

"Going?" inquired Redwood.

"I must get some beauty sleep," was her response.

"May I see you home?"

"Distinctly, no."

"Honoria," he pleaded, "will you always treat me in this manner?"

"I haven't the least idea what the future has in store for me, or for you," she answered. "You will recollect a certain night when we met in Chudleigh Woods?"

"Why will you always dwell upon that? Have I not admitted my blindness? Have I not begged you a thousand times to forgive me?"

"I have never told you, I think," she said, "that I was near putting an end to myself that night, nor how I was prevented and saved?"

"No, you have never told me, nor do I wish to hear. Forget it, once and for all."

"I can never forget it. I can see myself
standing on the little wooden bridge, looking
down into the lily pond. I can see the re-
flection of myself—" He had opened a bottle
of champagne, and he handed her a glass.
She took it from him, and gazed upon the
sparkling bubbles, but did not drink. "I
will tell you some day. . . . I was in rags,
and almost starving. Very different from now,
Austin"—a singular smile crossed her lovely
lips as she addressed him by the old name—
"I beg your pardon, I was forgetting—Redwood, I mean."

"Have done," he cried, tossing off a glass
of champagne, which increased the fever of
thirst that was on him. "You have punished
me sufficiently for my fault."

"Do you know," she continued, relentlessly,
"that I walked all the way from London to
see you—I told you at the time, I remember, and you said, how I must have
enjoyed myself. I threatened to expose you,
and you asked who would take the word of a
thief and a wanton against that of a gentle-

man ? You were right, Redwood. I did not know the world then. I know it now. Yes, I was not only a wanton ; I was a thief ; and yet you knew well I was neither. Give me your opinion of your conduct."

" It was brutal," he said sullenly.

" It was that, at least ; the word is too mild. . . . I was in rags ; the soles were worn off my feet ; despair was in my soul ; death seemed my only refuge ! "

" For God's sake," he cried, " talk of something else ! "

" But I want to remind you, Redwood," she said, putting down her untasted glass of champagne. " You said the little comedy in which we played the principal parts was finished. Why, Redwood, it was only the first act that was over ; even now it is not finished."

She was suddenly interrupted. From the stage came a scream of agony, answered by shrieks from the pit. Instinctively they moved to the front of the box.

CHAPTER XXXI.

THE cries of pain and alarm were caused by an accident to a small band of acrobats who had been doing their "turn." Two athletic men, lying on their backs with their legs raised in the air, had been tossing a diminutive boy from one to the other on the soles of their feet. The most difficult part of the boy's performance consisted in his being sent flying upwards by one of the men, and in his alighting in a standing position on the soles of the other man's feet. Before he alighted he had to turn a double somersault. He had twice missed his mark, and as it is a point of professional honour not to relinquish an act till it is accomplished, the boy was sent flying in the air a third time. But the little fellow by this time was exhausted and bewildered, and after turning the first somersault and a part of the second he fell in a heap, his head striking the stage. Having given utterance to his sharp scream of agony he became insensible. The answering shrieks in the pit had proceeded from his mother.

When Honoria and Louis Redwood reached the front of their box, the two elder acrobats were bending over the boy, the curtain was being lowered, the mother was clambering over the pit seats towards the stage, and the whole house was in confusion. The doctor in the opposite private box, which was on the pit tier, had made known that he was a medical man, and was being assisted along the cushions to the stage.

Honoria, who had been behind the scenes of the Royal Palace of Pleasure, knew that the wretched dressing rooms of this music hall could only be reached by means of a long narrow spiral staircase, and that it would be a matter of time and difficulty to carry the sufferer to a place where he could be properly attended to. She said hurriedly to Redwood,

33*

"Let him be brought up here; there is better accommodation and more room."

Redwood disappeared through a door at the side of the box which led to the stage, the free privilege of going behind the scenes and mixing with the performers being generally granted to those who occupied the principal box in the Palace of Pleasure.

Honoria, after seeing that the sofa in the adjoining spacious room was free, waited at the door, through which, presently, the boy was carried. The doctor and his friends, the woman from the pit, and the two acrobats in their tights and fleshings, accompanied him. While the boy was being attended to, the manager of the music hall made his appearance upon the stage, and said he was happy to inform the audience that the lad was not seriously injured, and that the performance would be continued; and immediately afterwards the band struck up the tune of one of the most popular songs of the day.

"Is he much hurt?" asked Honoria, of the doctor.

"A rib is broken," was the answer. "It will be best to take him to a hospital."

But, against this proposal the woman from the pit, who was the boy's mother, violently protested. The boy should be taken home to her own lodgings, she said, and no one else should nurse and look after him. They strove to persuade her to adopt the more sensible course, but she would not be persuaded, and as her right to decide could not be disputed they were compelled to let her have her way. It appeared that the boy, a mere child about eight years of age, was comparatively new to the business, and had been hired out by the mother, a very poor woman, to the two acrobats, against whom nothing could be urged except that they were following a dangerous occupation. They were very much concerned at the accident, and were ruefully contemplating the prospect of having to break their engagements.

"You said there wasn't a bit of danger," said the mother to them, with flaming eyes, "when you persuaded me to let you have him. I wish I'd bit my tongue off before I said yes."

" It ain't our fault, mother," said one of the men. " You jest ask him when he comes to whether we knocked him about, and whether he didn't like us. If he'd been my own brother he couldn't have been better treated. It licks me how it ever happened "

Redwood wondered at the interest Honoria was taking in "the confounded affair," but he did not venture to express himself to that effect. The gentlemen from the opposite box all inwardly commended Honoria, and if any one had hard thoughts of her they were much softened by her behaviour on this occasion. Redwood had opened a couple of bottles of champagne in lieu of something better to do, but only he and the two acrobats drank. A little brandy for the lad had been sent for.

" How's he getting on ? " asked the manager of the hall, coming into the room.

" He'll get over it," replied the doctor, " with care and nursing." He rose to his feet, and said to Honoria, "I can do nothing more for him at present. He should be got home and put to bed as soon as possible."

"Will it be a long job, sir?" inquired one of the acrobats.

"It is impossible to say," replied the doctor, "but he will not be fit for your kind of work again."

The men nodded gravely and departed.

"I will take the poor fellow home in my carriage," said Honoria to the mother, "if you won't mind."

"Mind, miss!" exclaimed the grateful woman. "God bless you for it. You've got a heart, you have."

"Will you come with us?" asked Honoria, addressing the doctor.

"If you wish," he said.

"I shall feel obliged. It will be a relief and a satisfaction to his mother. Excuse me for saying that I make myself responsible for everything." These last words were uttered to him aside.

"There will be no expense so far as I am

concerned," he said, gazing with curiosity and interest at her. "I shall be happy to attend to him till he is able to get about again."

"You are very good."

The doctor turned to his companions, with whom he had promised to spend the evening. They were to sup with him after the entertainment was over.

"We will follow in a cab," said the soldier, "and wait outside for you."

Honoria glanced at him, and the colour came into his face. It was he who carried the boy down to the carriage, and lifted him in. The mother and the doctor then stepped in, and after them Honoria.

"What are we to do, lady fair?" inquired Major Causton, who stood with Louis Redwood at the door of the carriage.

Redwood was sullen and savage; Honoria seemed to ignore his existence.

"I am not at all interested in what you do," said Honoria, as she gave the mother's address to her coachman, who drove away at a slow pace as he was directed, in order that the boy should not be jolted.

Major Causton looked at Louis Redwood and burst into a loud laugh.

"Damn you," cried Redwood, "What are you laughing at?"

"At myself," said Causton, heartily, "and you, and her, and the world in general. She's an original. I shouldn't wonder if she turned Sister of Mercy in the end. That woman, Redwood, is capable of anything."

"If ever I get hold of her again," muttered Redwood, "I'll make her pay for it."

Major Causton lit a cigar, and Redwood followed suit.

"She's a match for half a dozen of us," said the Major, eyeing his companion thoughtfully. "I've seen something of women, but she puzzles me. Hanged if I can make out whether she's bad or good at the bottom."

"You have nothing to complain of," observed Redwood; "you are in favour just now. It's Major this, and Major that, and

Major t'other with her all the time I happen
to be by."

"That's where it is," rejoined the Major,
"all the time you happen to be by. She
plays me off against you, dear boy. Don't
you see? She's got you tight by the gills,
and she knows how to play her line if ever
woman did. She has cost you a pretty penny,
Redwood. That's where I have the advantage
of you. You are rich; I am poor. I get my
sport for nothing."

"Sport, you call it!" exclaimed Redwood,
savagely. "Infernal torture, that's what it
is."

"You take things too seriously, dear boy.
Look at me. Nothing puts me out. Lady
fair smiles at me; I smile in return. She
frowns at me; I shrug my shoulders. Be
easy with her, as I am."

"I can't; it's not in my nature. When I
set my heart upon a thing I grow savage,
reckless, and I'm carried on against my will."

"You're changed from what you were, dear
boy. Not long since it would have been hard

to match you for coolness. Now you're losing
your head, and all through a woman. I say,
what did you mean by saying if ever you get
hold of her again! That 'again' opens a
chapter of past history. Was there ever
anything between you and lady fair?"

"That's my business. Mind your own."

"Thanks for the hint. I will. And that
reminds me that I'm in a tight fix just now.
Cleaned out at baccarat last night, and my
I. O. U.s flying all over the shop. Can you
spare fifty, dear boy?"

"I'll give you a cheque for it," said
Redwood readily.

"You're a prince with your money, dear
boy," said Causton admiringly. "It is right
that men like you should have it to spend.
But don't go the pace too fast. For my sake,
dear boy, for my sake. Can't afford to let
you get knocked over; should mourn it
deeply. What do you stand to lose on your
horse to-morrow?"

"Nothing. The horse can't lose. How
did Honoria get that infernal stuff into her

head about Morning Glory being first and Abracadabra second ? "

" How does she get anything into her head ? Do you suppose she takes me into her confidence ? It may look like it, but it's not the case. I've been taking the odds for her on both events—there was no harm in that. If I hadn't done it she would have shown me the door, and got some other fellow to do it."

" You might have let me into the secret," said Redwood, gloomily.

" Didn't dare to, dear boy. She swore me to secrecy. I give you my honest word, she made me take a Bible oath to it. It would have been dangerous to throw out a hint to you, dear boy. You can't keep your own counsel; you would have let the cat out of the bag. She's drawn you out a dozen times without you knowing it, to discover whether I'd been blabbing."

" I dare say you're right. It's true, I suppose, about the money she stands to win on her fancy ? "

" True as gospel, dear boy."

" She must have got a tip from some one. Have you any idea of the man?"

" I've no idea at all on the subject. She's got any number of tips from any number of people. All of us have. It's what brings so many of us to grief. My impression is that she is acting on her own fancy entirely, and she's not quite a fool, dear boy."

" She's a fool in this matter, as she'll find out before this time to-morrow."

" Well, the loss won't hurt her much," said Major Causton: " either way she wins a good stake. I suppose Beane's all right."

Beane was the name of the jockey who was to ride Abracadabra.

" Damn him!" cried Redwood. " Who can tell? There's about one in ten of the whole lot of them that a man can feel safe with. They're too much for us in the long run, Causton."

" They are, dear boy. Here we are at the club."

As they stepped to the door a man in a maudlin condition passed by, singing :

> " Abracadabra,
> Abracadabra,
> Abracadabra
> Has got 'em on toast."

" There's fame for you, dear boy," said the Major, laughing.

CHAPTER XXXII

HONORIA IN A NEW CHARACTER.

" The little fellow is comfortable now," said the doctor, " and I think he will do very well."

" Will you come to-morrow, sir ? " asked the anxious mother.

" Yes, I will see him in the morning. I will drop in on my way to the station. You are going, I suppose ? " He put this question to Honoria as he drew on his gloves.

" To the Derby ? " she said. " Oh, yes."

" I saw the owner of Abracadabra in your box. They say the horse is certain to win."

" That is what he says himself. Have you backed it ? "

" I throw away a few sovereigns every year," he replied, with a smile. " on the Derby and the Leger, but I never put them on till the morning of the race."

" I fancy Morning Glory," said Honoria.

" Do you ? I shall divide my investment, then."

" Good-night," said Honoria, holding out her hand.

" Can I not see you to your carriage ? "

- " No ; I shall remain here a little while."

They shook hands, and he went down to his friends, who were waiting for him in the street.

" That woman is incomprehensible," he said to them as they walked away. " I never witnessed greater kindness than she is showing to those poor people."

" One has only to look in her face," said the soldier, " to know what she is. You promised to relate her history." This to the editor.

" To a certain extent it is wrapped in mystery," said the editor, " which makes it all the more piquant. What I know of it is from hearsay. You must promise not to quarrel with me."

" I promise," said the soldier. " I can believe as much of it as I please."

" To be sure you can. I am not certain as to when Honoria appeared in our social firmament, but she has been common talk for some time past. Where she hails from no one appears to know. It is said that Mr. Redwood, the owner of the favourite for the Derby, could let in a light upon it if he chose. Whether that is so or not I cannot say myself. She appears to be on intimate terms with him."

" If I am a judge of signs," said the soldier, " he appears to be forcing his company upon her. It is evident to me that she regards him with aversion."

" That may be. Nevertheless, scandal couples them together, and there is no doubt that he is pursuing her with his attentions."

" By the way," interrupted the doctor, " she advised me to back Morning Glory, to-morrow."

" I shall take her tip," said the editor, " believing Mr. Redwood to be capable of any trickery."

" I am with you there," said the soldier.

" Of course you are. He is not the only victim to her charms. There are a dozen infatuated gentlemen ready to throw their fortunes into her lap. I am not in a position to say that she gives them encouragement ; if she holds them off it makes the pursuit the hotter, as probably she knows."

" I cannot commend you for fairness," said the soldier, who was listening with evident impatience and disapproval. " You assert that you are acquainted with particulars, and in proof of this you are regaling us with tittle-tattle. You have heard this, you have heard that. You are not in a position to say this, you are not in a position to say that, and yet, upon such an admission of ignorance, you make remarks which tend to place this lady in a bad light. It is a fashionable method of blasting character."

" My dear sir," said the editor, with mock solemnity, " would you turn a deaf ear to the voice of scandal ? "

" An absolutely deaf ear," replied the soldier, indignantly, " when the strongest

evidence that can be brought to support it
is the kind of stuff which you can retail
out."

The editor was nettled. " Have you ever
seen a lady in such a position as you have
seen Honoria this evening? " he asked.

" You mean," said the soldier, " occupying
a private box in a notorious music hall, in the
company of men of doubtful reputation? I
admit I should not like to see my sister there,
but I believe that ladies of whom you would
not presume to speak disrespectfully have
been seen in music halls in the society of men
not famous for morality. There were plenty
of respectable women in the Palace of
Pleasure, in pit and gallery and circle : why
should the circumstance of one appearing in
a private box make her infamous? "

" There is no arguing with this modern
Don Quixote," observed the editor, recovering
his good humour, " whose chivalrous defence
almost converts me. But, indeed, I am by
no means unkindly disposed towards Honoria,
and I am inclined to overlook her faults

because of her virtues and her commendable qualities."

" Let us have a review of these," said the soldier.

" Report says that when she first burst upon society she was not remarkable for education. Since that time she has undergone a most wonderful improvement. Engaging capable tutors, she has learned to play, to sing, to draw, and to speak modern languages, no worse and no better perhaps than the ordinary modern young lady of fashion."

" That falsifies the presumption that she has a vicious mind."

" I thoroughly agree with you. It is not her mind, but her antecedents——"

" Of which you know nothing."

" The antecedents which vague rumour ascribes to her, and also the style in which she lives, keeping horses, carriages, servants, all contribute to the scandal which, justly or unjustly, attaches to her name. On the other hand, it is known that she is charitable ; she gives to the poor, she contributes to deserving

institutions. Upon the whole, if I commenced
with the intention of traducing Honoria I
have made a bad case of it, as you will
admit. If she ever comes to grief I, for
one, shall be sorry to hear it. I hope," he
said, turning to the soldier, "I have made
amends."

" What you have said," replied the soldier,
" strengthens the good opinion I have of her.
There is not a lady in the land who could
have acted more kindly than she did towards
that poor lad who met with the accident.
And now you must all come with me, and
have a bit of supper."

And the incident being thus pleasantly
terminated, they plunged into other topics
upon which there was no divergence of
opinion.

These gentlemen were not the only persons
who were talking together on this night of
Honoria and the unveiled story of our life.
Our old friends, Mr. Millington and Mr.
Barlow, were among the audience in the
Royal Palace of Pleasure. They had come

in late, just as the accident occurred, and had seen Honoria lean forward over her box.

"There's Honoria," said Mr. Barlow, "and Mr. Redwood with her. She is sending him away. What for, I wonder?"

They soon learned the reason. The news of Honoria's kindness quickly passed through the house, and reached their ears.

"She's a trump, that woman," said Mr. Barlow. "I saw her carriage in front. Let us go and see what she's up to."

Mr. Barlow was a privileged person; he had free admission to many places of entertainment, the Royal Palace of Pleasure being among them. By virtue of this privilege he conveyed Mr. Millington to the back of the boxes, and there they witnessed something of what has already been described, and heard the rest. Without being themselves observed they followed Honoria and the boy's mother, and the little band of gentlemen who had been present while the doctor was attending to the little fellow. Standing near the carriage they heard the address of the poor woman given to the coachman—No. 7, Wellington Street, South Lambeth.

"That's curious," said Mr. Barlow, as the carriage drove away. "Was it No. 7, Millington?"

"Yes," replied Mr. Millington, "that was the number. Why is it curious?"

"I'll tell you presently; it will interest you."

His attention was now centred upon Mr. Louis Redwood and Major Causton, who were standing on the curb, looking after the carriage. He had heard the Major's laugh and Mr. Redwood's angry exclamation.

"She has left them out in the cold," said Mr. Barlow, chuckling, "and friend Redwood is ready to cut somebody's throat. There's an instance of retributive justice, Millington, whether you believe in it or not. The man who made Honoria what she is, and would have laughed to see her starve and rot, would give every shilling he has in the world to make her his slave again."

"You don't believe he has any hold on her now?" asked Mr. Millington.

"No more than I have; less I should say. It's she that's got a hold on him. She has been playing with him ever since that night we saw her at the theatre, when he made up to her and she gave him a look I can see now. It was when you gave up the Haldane commission, you know."

"Yes," said Mr. Millington, "I remember the night. You took me in the afternoon to Rotten Row, where Honoria was riding."

"That's the time. From that day to this she's been leading him a dance, and she has played her game so cleverly that he has become almost desperate. Who would have thought she had such a head? I would give something to see her ruin him completely—and it's on the cards, Millington, it's on the cards."

"Why doesn't he give her up?"

"He can't. He has never been fought in this way before, and the longer the battle goes on the madder he grows, and the keener his longing to become her master once more. He has been able to do as he liked with other women, but this one keeps him at bay. I call it a fine revenge."

"She takes his money, I've heard," said Millington.

"She does, and laughs openly in his face all the time. It's my opinion she would like to see his horse beaten to-morrow. There's nothing that woman wouldn't do to humiliate and madden him. Millington, I've a fancy to go to 7, Wellington Street, just to reconnoitre. Will you come with me?"

"With pleasure. George is out courting, and will not be home till late, so I shall not be missed."

"Ah," said Mr. Barlow, "that's a long engagement between him and pretty Rachel Diprose. We haven't been much together lately, you and I, Millington, and we have plenty of things to talk about. They're pretty constant to each other, those two, but is it likely ever to come to anything?"

"I hope so," replied Mr. Millington, "and

so do they, of course. Though, for obstinacy,
and sticking to her word, there's not a girl
within a hundred miles of us to equal Rachel.
Says George to her, 'Don't let us wait any
longer, Rachel. I'm in a position to maintain
a home, so let us go to church, and get it
over.' 'No, George,' says the steadfast
young woman, 'I've made a vow never to get
married till my dear mistress is settled, and I
mean to stick to it. You're a foolish fellow
to keep yourself tied to a girl like me. Look
out for another wife, George, and let us
shake hands and say good-bye to each other.'
Of course George won't listen to anything of
the sort ; he makes himself as cheerful as he
can be under the circumstances, and says
that nothing but death shall part them. Miss
Haldane does her best to persuade Rachel to
do as George wishes, but Rachel won't give
way. And so it goes on. I don't like to see
George and Rachel wasting the best part
of their lives, but it can't be helped it
seems. There's no understanding women,
Barlow."

"It's difficult, I grant," said Mr. Barlow, contemplatively; "they have ways of their own, but they're not always wrong. How is Miss Haldane getting along?"

"She and Rachel make just enough to live upon. I suspect she would be in sore straits if Rachel left her."

"That's what makes one admire Rachel. It's hard lines for George, but if the marriage ever comes off, she'll make him a rare good wife. How is Miss Haldane's sweethearting getting along?"

"About the same as Rachel's. Young Mr. Palmer, you know, went to Australia to make his fortune, and came back poorer than he went. He is going to make a great name one day, they say, but at present he and his father just manage to rub along. But when things are brighter with them, which I've an idea will be the case before long, Miss Haldane's promise to her father that she will not marry without his consent, is likely to stop the way. Everything," said Mr. Millington, passing his hand across his forehead with an air of vexation, "seems to be in a tangle. I give up thinking of them sometimes."

"Talk of the devil!" cried Mr. Barlow, looking after a man who was crossing the road.

"What's the matter?" inquired Mr. Millington.

"This is a night of coincidences," replied Mr. Barlow, 'and I believe in coincidences. Do you see that gentleman there?"

"That one shambling along on the other side? What of him?"

"It is Mr. Haldane himself. He has come back. What little game will he be up to now?"

Mr. Millington ran across, and passing the gentleman spoken of without drawing attention upon himself, returned to Mr. Barlow.

"It's Mr. Haldane, sure enough. You know more about him than I do. Let me into the secret, Barlow."

"There isn't much of a secret about it," said Mr. Barlow. "When the Chudleigh estate fell into the hands of Mr. Redwood, our fine gentleman there made himself scarce. Went abroad and kept there. Now, he's back again."

"He may have been in London some time, for all you know."

"I think not. Although that commission I was engaged on for Mrs. Kennedy fell through, I have kept myself posted up as well as I could with everyone concerned in it. You will recollect that I thought it the most interesting case I ever had to do with."

"You never told me why it fell through, Barlow."

"It's soon told. At the time Mrs. Kennedy put the case into my hands she had money. What did the foolish lady do but allow herself to be persuaded to invest the whole of her little fortune in some South American mine. Crash went the concern, and swallowed up every shilling she had. She came to me with tears in her eyes, and said she could not prosecute the matter any further. She was in my debt over £50, and she owes the money still. There being no funds, I could not go on, of

course, and there was an end of the affair so
far as I was concerned. Of all the men and
women we got to know through your commission for Mr. Haldane and mine for Mrs.
Kennedy, only two have managed to keep
themselves afloat — Mr. Redwood and
Honoria. It was a terrible come down for
the Haldanes, but I've an impression we
haven't seen the end of it. Here we are in
Wellington Street. There's Honoria's carriage
waiting at the door of No. 7. That's what I
mean by a coincidence. In that very house
lives Mrs. Kennedy and her adopted daughter,
Adeline Ducroz. You can't have forgotten
those remarkable letters of hers I gave you
to read?"

"It isn't likely I could forget them. How
do these two ladies live?"

"Mrs. Kennedy takes in needlework, and
they starve on it."

"What does the other one do?"

"Drink. You know what a dipsomaniac
is, Millington?";

"Yes."

"That is what Adeline Ducroz is—that is what she was when Mr. Haldane under the assumed name of Julius Clifford, deserted her in Paris—that is what she was when she was wandering through the Continent. She is now irreclaimable. All Mrs. Kennedy's efforts to cure her of the awful habit— which is more common than you suppose— have ended in failure. But the good lady has not abandoned her; she has undertaken a terrible responsibility, and does not shrink from it. She works for the lost creature day and night, nurses her, watches over her as well as she is able to, and still hopes against hope. It is a dreadful burden."

"I can imagine nothing more dreadful," said Mr. Millington. "Barlow, if I don't mistake, you once had an idea that Miss Haldane was Adeline Ducroz's daughter?"

"I did."

"Are you of the same opinion still?"

"Upon my word," said Mr. Barlow, looking up at the windows of No. 7, "I hardly know what to think. I have seen Adeline Ducroz on several occasions, and I can see no likeness between them. But Adeline Ducroz as a woman and a confirmed drunkard, and Adeline Ducroz as a young girl in whom the awful vice was absent, must be two different beings. To see her as she is can give one no idea of what she was, and it seems a crime to associate so sweet a lady as Miss Haldane with a creature so lost and degraded. Here is Mrs. Kennedy coming out of the house now."

A grey-haired woman, her face lined with care, issued from the door of No. 7. She carried a bundle, and after an anxious upward glance was walking away when Mr. Barlow stepped forward and accosted her. Not many words passed between them, but Mr. Millington saw Mr. Barlow slip something into her hand.

"She has just finished a dress for a private customer," said Mr. Barlow, rejoining his friend, "which must be delivered to-night. She is in great anxiety because she fears she may be kept out late. She says she left her daughter asleep, but she is not easy in her mind about her. It is supposed in the neighbourhood that they are really mother and daughter. Another proof of her wonderful kindness to the lost woman."

"If she is in a drunken sleep," said Mr. Millington, "it is likely she will not soon awake."

"If she is," said Mr. Barlow. "That's where the doubt comes in. You have no notion of the cunning of these dipso-maniacs. One is never safe with them. The odds are that she is only pretending to be asleep so as to get her protector out of the way."

"What would be the good of that? She has no money to obtain liquor."

"Oh, she'll beg, borrow, or steal it, or perhaps take something from the room to sell for gin. Let us be jogging, Millington. We shall do no good remaining here. It is kind of Honoria to stop with that poor little fellow who met with the accident. By-and-by, old fellow, when the account is reckoned up, there's many a good deed will be set down to the credit of the woman that scoundrel Redwood brought to shame. Come along "

CHAPTER XXXIII.

ADELINE DUCROZ.

It was very near midnight before Honoria prepared to take her departure. She had done much in the meantime to assuage the mother's anxiety, and to make things easy for her and the injured lad. Impressing into her service a slatternly girl who lived in the house with her parents, Honoria had sent her out half-a-dozen times to purchase what was required. Every time the girl went out Honoria discovered something else that was wanting, and every time she came back she was sent out again to obtain it. The pleasure Honoria conferred by her kindness was nothing compared to the pleasure she derived from administering it. She moved about the room as if she had lived in it all her life, and as if she were quite accustomed

35*

to that kind of existence. The mother, who rejoiced in no less common name than Smith, for the most part looked on in wonder at Honoria's proceedings. The lad opening his eyes once or twice, also gazed in wonder at the beautifully - dressed lady until fatigue caused him to close them again; finally he fell into a sound slumber, from which he was not likely to awake till morning. Between whiles Honoria had extracted from Mrs. Smith the whole of her history. She was a widow with one child, and being very poor had consented to let the acrobats have him for a term of years upon an ascending scale of wages, commencing at four shillings a week. The lad was nearly at the end of his first year, and upon his four shillings a week, which she received regularly, and as much charing as she could obtain, his mother managed to live.

"It is a hard life," said Honoria pityingly.

"It is hard," said Mrs. Smith, "but it might be worse. My Jack's spoilt for his trade now, poor boy, by what the doctor said.

He was so fond of it, too. He commenced tumbling about when he was two years old, and before he was three I was always catching him standing on his head. He got regularly talked about, and people called him the little clown. Those men got to hear of him, and when they came and offered to take and teach him the business I thought it was as good a thing as could happen to him. It's hard to know what to do with one's children, but I'm glad he's a boy instead of a girl."

"Yes," said Honoria, looking steadily at the mother, "you are right to be glad of that."

She listened to a noise without, the voice of some creature shrieking out a song, the words of which were not distinguishable.

"You'd get used to that noise," remarked Mrs. Smith, "if you lived in the house. Don't let it trouble you. It's only Mrs. Kennedy's daughter."

"It does not trouble me," said Honoria, "but there is something very pitiful in the sound. Mrs. Kennedy's daughter! Surely not a young girl?"

"Oh, no, a woman as old as I am, but I'm thankful that I'm not like her."

"Is she sober?"

"I don't know. She never is if she can help it. When she's not sober, she's mad."

"Always?"

"Nearly always. I've seen her two or three times as near in her right senses as she's ever likely to be, and I've fairly started at the change in her."

"In what respect?"

"Well, if you'll believe me, she was more of a lady at those times than any of us. Quiet too, and well-spoken. There was once when Mrs. Kennedy managed to keep her right for nearly a week, and if you'd seen her then you'd have pitied and wondered at her. But there! A kind lady like you would be ready to pity anyone in misfortune."

"Never mind that. What I have done has been to please myself. I am glad I was

at the theatre to-night when your boy met
with his accident."

"You mean the music-hall," Mrs. Smith
said, and then hesitated. When her son was
carried up to the room adjoining Honoria's
private box she had not caught the name of
the lady who had proved so kind to her, her
anxiety rendering her deaf to everything but
her boy's danger. The whole of the time
Honoria had been with her in the one room
she occupied in this humble house she had
not addressed her as "Miss" or "Madam,"
being doubtful which would be right. It was
this doubt that caused her to hesitate now,
and Honoria, understanding that she had not
completed the sentence, looked at her with a
smile. "May I take the liberty of asking,"
said Mrs. Smith, "whether you are a married
lady ?"

"I am not married," replied Honoria, very
readily.

"That's what's been bothering me, whether
I ought to call you Miss or not. You can't
be more glad, Miss, that you were at the

music-hall to-night than we've got occasion
to be. My boy couldn't help meeting with
the accident, I suppose. What is to be, will
be ; and as it was to happen, your being there
was a windfall to us—though I can't quite
make out, Miss, why you ought to be glad."

"Can you understand," asked Honoria,
"that it is a real pleasure when one woman
can help another ? "

"You mean, Miss, when a rich lady can
help a poor woman ? "

"If you like to put it that way, yes."

"That's one way of looking at it certainly,
but it only proves more and more what a
kind heart you've got. There's that Mrs.
Kennedy's daughter going it again. Just
listen to her."

Honoria stood at the door a moment or
two, listening to the wild singing, some words
of which came now to her ear.

"Why," she cried, "she's singing a French
song."

"She can do that, Miss, and talk other
foreign languages ; and so can her mother.

It's a sad pity they've come down so low. It
isn't half as bad when you're born to it;
then you don't expect much, and you get
accustomed to things, but to be born well off
and accustomed to having everything you
want, and then to come down to poverty's
door—I can understand how hard it must be,
though it isn't my own case. I don't know,
Miss, whether you see it as I do."

" Why shouldn't I be able to see it as you
do ? " asked Honoria.

" Well, Miss," replied Mrs. Smith, her
admiring eyes taking in every detail of
Honoria's dress and beauty, " it's easy to see
you've never known want."

" Have I not ? " said Honoria, with a
singular smile. " Are you something of a
fortune-teller, then ? "

" I can tell your fortune by the cards,"
said Mrs. Smith.

" Which is sure to come true," observed
Honoria.

The woman laughed. " Sometimes it does,
sometimes it doesn't. That's as it happens."

"Never mind the future," said Honoria. "Tell me about the past—my past. I have never known want?"

"I should say that's certain, Miss."

"A lady born?"

"Yes, Miss."

"Just think. Do ladies go to such places as we met in to-night?"

"Why not, Miss? I'm a respectable woman, poor as I am, and I go into the pit—with an order, Miss; I couldn't afford to pay. You're a lady and you go into the swell parts. Fine feathers make fine birds, they say, and most people believe it. I don't. If you don't know how to wear the feathers, you're soon found out. If I dressed myself as a lady, having the chance that'll never come to me, why, they'd spot me at once. 'You a lady!' they'd cry. Now, there's Mrs. Kennedy and her daughter. Here they are, living upon next to nothing; they've got the worst rooms in the house, an attic at the top, and I don't suppose after paying the rent, that they've more than six or seven shillings

a week to live upon. They've been in want
of a crust they have. But for all that,
and though they've got no more clothes
than they stand upright in — and they're
nothing to brag of — you couldn't mistake
that they were born ladies, and brought
up so. If they were to come into money
to-morrow, and the daughter would only
keep from drink, they would know how
to wear their fine feathers—just as you do,
Miss."

"Tell me something more about these poor
ladies," said Honoria, earnestly. " Mrs.
Kennedy works for a living?"

"As hard as the hardest of us; stops up
half the night sewing, when she can get it to
do."

"Sewing! Has she a sewing machine?"

" A sewing machine! Why, where should
she get one from without a farthing in her
pocket?"

"I forgot. And she stops up working
half the night, stitching, stitching—there's a
song about that I dare say you've heard of.

And though she works so hard the wolf is always at their door?"

"That's it, Miss. They're happy ones who've never seen the beast."

"Like me," said Honoria, smiling again.

"Yes, Miss, like you."

"I must be going now; you must try and get some rest." She slipped a half-sovereign into the woman's hand. "Is there anything more I can do for you?"

"You've done all you could, Miss," said Mrs. Smith, with tears in her eyes, "and I don't know how to thank you."

"Don't try. My visit has done me more good than it has you."

"It's a pity there's not more like you, Miss."

A smothered sound, half sob, half laugh, escaped from Honoria, but she was quite calm and composed almost in the same breath.

"You may be wrong there," she said, taking up her gloves.

"No, Miss; I'm right; but it's like you

to make light of what you've done. Shall
we see you again?"

"Not to-morrow; I shall be busy; the day
after. Good-night."

": Good-night, Miss, and God bless you."

Honoria, closing the door behind her, did
not go downstairs to her carriage, but upstairs to the attic, in which Mrs. Kennedy's
daughter was still singing fitfully, but more
softly now. The stairs and passages were
dark, and she had to feel her way by the
balustrade. A human form, lying across the
stairs, impeded her progress, and started up
as it was touched by her foot.

" Who's that?" a voice enquired. It was
the slatternly girl she had employed to do
her errands.

"I am going up to Mrs. Kennedy's room,"
replied Honoria.

"Oh, it's you, lady! I'll show it yer."

"What are you lying on the stairs for?"
asked Honoria.

"To prevent 'er going out if I can," said
the girl, with an upward jerk of her thumb,

which Honoria could not see. " Mrs. Kennedy
gives me a ha'penny for it. She's a good sort
is Mrs. Kennedy. It ain't safe for 'er to go
out by 'erself." With another upward jerk
of her thumb.

" Why isn't it safe ? "

" She ain't to be trusted a minute by
'erself," whispered the girl. " Mrs. Kennedy's
afeerd she might do somebody a mischief."

" Is she violent, then ? I understood she
was harmless."

" She ain't done nothink up to now," said
the girl, still in a whisper, " but there's no
telling when she's going to begin. And she's
that artful ! "

If Honoria could have seen the girl's face
she would have seen an expression upon it
signifying that for artfulness the woman
upstairs had not her equal.

" Show me her room."

" Take 'old of me, and mind 'ow yer step.
There's 'oles in some of the stairs. The 'ouse
is coming to pieces, it is."

The room was as dark as the staircase, and

when Honoria entered it, which she did alone, the slatternly girl keeping by the open door, she could see nothing of its occupant.

"Go downstairs and ask Mrs. Smith to lend me a candle."

"Ain't you afeerd?"

"No, go at once."

The girl slid down by means of the creaking balustrade, and presently Mrs. Smith herself came up with a lighted candle.

"You can't do her any good," said the woman, shaking her head.

"Oblige me, and leave me alone with her."

"I'll wait outside."

Honoria taking the candle from her, closed the door.

A woman, crouching by the miserable mattress on the floor, peeped cunningly through her fingers as Honoria approached her. She was much older than Honoria had supposed her to be; her clothes were of the poorest description, but bore evidence of neat mending and patching; her grey hair, also, though she had it pulled over her face, where

it hung straggling down, must have been
regularly combed and brushed. The room
was clean and tidy ; it was a work, living, and
bedroom, all in one, and contained, for furniture, but two wooden chairs, a deal table, and
the bed on the floor, but there were no traces
of disorder apparent. In the dumb signs
that met Honoria's eyes there was no degradation, but distinct evidences of poverty
bravely borne. The degradation was in the
woman's face—a bloated face, with swollen
cheeks and lips, and bleared eyes. The hands
she held before it trembled and twitched ;
they were not the hands of one accustomed to
menial work ; they were small and shapely,
and in the woman's whole appearance, miserable and degraded as it was, there seemed to
Honoria to be a singular assumption that she
had not been always so low and vile as at the
present time.

"Are you ill ?" asked Honoria, pityingly.

The woman slowly removed her hands from
her face, and stroked Honoria's dress.

"Let me whisper to you," she said.

Honoria was startled by the voice. It was so thick and guttural, and so difficult to understand, that it sounded scarcely human.

"Speak out,' said Honoria, "there is no one near."

"There is," said the woman. "A devil is hiding—there in that corner!—he will come out when you are gone. He must not hear. Let me whisper." Honoria bent her head. "Are you a lady?"

"I am a woman, as you see."

"Have you money?"

"Yes."

"Give me a shilling. They starve me; they don't give me anything to eat. Give me a shilling."

"I will get you some food."

"I don't want food—I want a shilling. Give me sixpence. Look at me; I am shaking all over. I want medicine; I can go out and buy it. Give me twopence."

Honoria did not know immediately what to do. She felt that the degraded creature wanted the money for drink, and yet she

seemed impelled to give it to her. It was
only by an effort that she restrained the
unwholesome prompting.

"No," she said, "I will not give you
money."

The woman was evidently accustomed to
such refusals; she threw herself full length
on the floor, her face downwards, and begged
no more.

Honoria lingered a few moments in the
room; she was sincerely desirous to relieve
the poverty so plainly visible, but she could
not do it through this lost creature. On the
mantelshelf she saw a little stone bottle of ink,
and a pen by its side; there was also a worn
blotting pad as she supposed. She took it
down and opened it. There was neither
writing paper nor envelope there; in their
place was a photograph which, though faded,
had seemingly been carefully preserved. It
was the portrait of a young woman, dark, and
full-blooded as she was herself. The sweetness of spring was in the face and eyes, but
it needed not that to render it beautiful. It

was one of those rare faces which, under
fortunate circumstances, would not lose its
attractiveness with advancing age. Honoria
gazed at it for many moments in silence.
This silence alarmed Mrs. Smith, who was
standing in the passage, waiting for Honoria.
She knocked at the door, and receiving no
answer, gently opened it and advanced into
the room. Honoria was so absorbed in the
picture that she did not turn her head; she
had not heard the opening of the door.

"What are you looking at, Miss?" asked
Mrs. Smith. Honoria, aroused to conscious-
ness, laid the portrait down. "Oh, the
picture," said Mrs. Smith. "You'd hardly
believe it was hers."

"Hers!" echoed Honoria, contemplating
the prostrate form. "Is it possible she was
ever like this?"

"It's her picture, taken when she was a
young woman. And now I look at you——"
But she paused suddenly, and snapped her
lips together. "Are you coming down, Miss.
You can't do any good here?"

36*

"You were saying," said Honoria, "'and now I look at you,' but you did not finish."

"It's nothing, Miss. I'll light you down."

"But I wish to hear what was in your mind. Oblige me, and complete the sentence. There can be no harm in it."

"Of course there's no harm in it," said Mrs. Smith, with a curious hesitation, "but it mightn't be exactly pleasant."

"Oblige me and say what you were about to say." She took the portrait in her hand again, and held it out to Mrs. Smith.

"I was going to say, if you'll forgive me for it, that it's not unlike you. It's a foolish fancy, and I don't know how it ever came in my head."

"I don't think it's fancy; it struck me as I was looking at it. Is it like Mrs. Kennedy, too?"

"Not a bit. Mrs. Kennedy is quite a different sort of woman. There's a good many that don't believe——" Again she broke off in the middle of a sentence. "We'd best talk downstairs," she said, in a low tone.

"You wouldn't think she was listening, but it's my belief she hears every word we say."

"Yes," said Honoria, "we will talk down-stairs."

She cast a last compassionate glance at the prostrate woman, and left the room with Mrs. Smith.

"They do say," she prompted——

"That there's no relationship at all between Mrs. Kennedy and the woman she calls her daughter."

"But why should she work for her as she does? Why does she make herself a slave for her?"

"There's the mystery. We don't worry ourselves about it. We've got enough troubles of our own."

"Yes, you must have. Can you give me a sheet of paper and an envelope?"

"Yes, Miss."

This is what Honoria wrote:

"One who sincerely sympathizes with Mrs. Kennedy, and is desirous to further assist her, requests her acceptance of the enclosed. In the course of a few days the writer will place herself in communication with Mrs. Kennedy."

The "enclosed" was a bank note for five pounds. Honoria fastened the envelope, and addressing it to Mrs. Kennedy, requested Mrs. Smith to give it to her upon her return home that night. It happened, as Honoria stood in the passage, about to take her departure, that the street door was opened with a latch-key, and a woman was heard ascending the stairs.

"That's Mrs. Kennedy's step," said Mrs. Smith.

" I do not wish her to know," said Honoria, " that it is I who left the note for her."

" Very well, Miss."

The light fell upon Honoria's face as Mrs. Kennedy came up to her, and a startled look flashed into the elder woman's eyes. She stood on the top of the stairs gazing at Honoria till she passed out of the house.

CHAPTER XXXIV.

MR. HALDANE RETURNS.

LOUIS REDWOOD and Major Causton went to a great many places that night, after Honoria had given them the cold shoulder, as the gallant major expressed it, and did not stop long in any. There was a certain theatre where Redwood, as a particular friend of the manager and lessee, was welcome behind the scenes, as at the Royal Palace of Pleasure, whenever he cared to show his face there, and as a matter of course any friend he took with him was also welcome. Redwood had seen a great deal of life, and was still seeing it, but it was only with its darker shadows that he was familiar. The theatre to which he took Major Causton owed a great deal to him, literally owed a great deal to him, for it was mainly by his cheques that it was kept going. Now-a-days many young gentlemen of fashion

and fortune think it the proper thing to do to
back a young actor who is ambitious to
blossom into a star, and in more cases than
one the result has been satisfactory. There
are other theatres, kept open by a layman's
money, in which the end to be obtained is not
so laudable, the aspirant therein being an
empty-headed female who imagines that a
very liberal display of her person will atone
for her lack of brains. It was in a theatre of
this kind that Redwood and the Major idled
away some twenty minutes. To do Louis
Redwood justice, he had no particular feeling
for the empty-headed female who ruled over
it ; he spent some of his money in a theatre
of this kind because it was accounted the
proper thing to do, as above stated, and
because anything of a higher aim, with an
intellectual end in view, would not have
suited his tastes.

"Why, here's Louis!" exclaimed the female
he was backing, when he and the Major made
their appearance. "How are you, old
chappie?"

Redwood, surveying her with the air of a master who is not too well pleased with his bargain, gave her an indolent nod, and drawled out,

"My friend, Major Causton."

"Glad to see you, Major," said the female, who was nothing if she was not vulgarly familiar with every man who enjoyed her polite society. She was what is termed a fine woman—that is, there was plenty of her. She was arrayed as Ganymede, and she made it a boast on certain gala nights that it was not stage wine she handed round, but real sparkling champagne. Truth to tell, she had about as much regard for Redwood as he had for her; she knew her reign was coming to an end, but it had served her purpose, for she had "hooked" a brainless swell, who had commenced to waste his fortune upon her, and who would go on recklessly doing so until he came face to face with ruin. This favoured one was behind the scenes when Redwood came in, and looked very black at what he deemed an intrusion. Redwood took no notice of him, however, and at the end of twenty minutes left the field.

"So far as I am concerned," he remarked to Major Causton, as they walked away, " the theatre will close next week. I am about sick of the affair."

" Wonder you ever had anything to do with it," said the Major.

" I made a promise," said Redwood, quietly, " and I stuck to it. I generally do, whatever the cost."

" When you make up your mind to a thing, dear boy, you generally do stick to it."

" It's my way ; I never give in."

They were both thinking of Honoria when they made these remarks, and the Major was debating who would win. It was a battle between them, he knew, though he did not quite understand the rights of it. Had he been pinned to a declaration he would have been inclined to back Honoria, for whose intel-lect, as well as for whose beauty, he had an intense admiration.

From the theatre they proceeded to two

clubs, of which both were members. In one
a Derby sweep was being drawn, the first
prize in which was a thousand pounds. As
they entered the room the name of " Mr.
Louis Redwood" was called out, and then the
horse was drawn—Abracadabra.

" By the Lord," exclaimed Major Causton,
" you're in luck, dear boy!"

A murmur ran round when it was seen
that the owner was present, and envious con-
gratulations were poured upon him. He took
it all very coolly; the lucky draw did not
stir him in the least.

"I should have been equally pleased," he
said, "if I had drawn a blank. Why did not
one of you fellows get my horse?"

" Here is my name called out," cried the
Major, excitedly. " A blank, of course."

But, no; he drew Morning Glory.

" Three cheers," he said, rubbing his hands.

" Will you change, Major?" asked Redwood.

Major Causton was about to say, " Done,"
but suddenly pulled himself up. " No, dear

boy," he replied. "Everybody will know I've drawn Morning Glory, and it will be almost like throwing Honoria over not to stand by the horse."

"As you please ; you will repent it."

"I hope so, for your sake," said the Major, rather ruefully, Redwood's tone was so con- fident. "I shall be satisfied if I'm placed."

Upon leaving the second club they visited Redwood expressed his intention of going home, saying he had had too many late nights the last week or two, and wanted to be fresh for the morning.

"I have to drive Honoria down, you know," he said.

"You might do the amiable, dear boy, and invite me ; it will be better than going down by rail."

"O, you can come ; there will be room for you on the drag."

"Thanks," said the delighted Major, always ready to enjoy himself at another man's expense. "By this time to-morrow night we shall know where we are."

They parted at the door of Redwood's chambers, where our old friend Simpson, who had taken service with him after Mr. Haldane had gone to the wall, was arranging certain matters for the drive to Epsom. Simpson had changed very little, except that he was slyer and sleeker than ever; his foxlike eyes looked up as his master entered the room.

" Give me some champagne and Appolinaris, Simpson."

" Yes, sir."

Redwood did not usually treat his champagne so, but he wanted a long drink, and it was the most harmless he could take Simpson waited until he had emptied the glass, and then said :

" There's been somebody here to see you, sir."

" A lady ? "

" No sir, a gentleman," said Simpson, with a sly smile.

" Let him go to the devil," said Redwood.

" Yes, sir," said Simpson, and said no more. He was by this time well acquainted

with his master's moods, and never opposed
them.

Louis Redwood lit a cigar, and paced the
room.

" Everything will be right in the morning ? "
he said, presently.

" Everything, sir."

" Take care that it is, or look out for
yourself."

" Yes, sir."

Redwood was in a brutal humour, but his
valet was not to be ruffled. Simpson was
quite comfortable ; he had a substantial sum
in the bank. The service he had taken with
Louis Redwood had proved a lucrative one ;
the wages were good, the perquisites better,
the pilferings best. He would not have wept
if he were suddenly discharged, though he
would have preferred to hold on a little
longer. He had, of course, backed " Abracadabra " for the Derby ; he had the firmest
faith in his master's horse, and thought, with
numbers of others, that it could not lose the
race. He stood to win five hundred pounds,

and looked upon the money as already in his pocket.

"What did you say about a gentleman calling?" asked Redwood, when he had smoked his cigar through.

"He wanted to see you very particularly, sir."

"Anyone I know?"

"Oh, yes, sir; an old friend of yours." He added, under his bated breath, "and of mine."

"An old friend," said Redwood. "Where's his card?"

"He didn't leave one, sir. He left his name."

"What is it?"

"Mr. Haldane, sir."

Redwood stopped in his walk. "He is in England, then. When did he come back?"

"I don't know, sir. I didn't ask him. He said he wanted to see you very particularly, and asked me if you would be home to-night"

"Yes, go on," said Redwood impatiently.

" Don't chop it up into bits. Out with the lot."

" I said, sir, you might and you mightn't, and then he said he would call again, and take his chance of finding you. There's the bell, sir. It might be him."

Redwood reflected a moment. "If it is Mr. Haldane, show him in."

" Yes, sir."

" And look here, Simpson. When he's here you can pack yourself off. I shan't want you again to-night. If I catch you peeping through keyholes and listening, I'll break your neck."

" Yes, sir," said Simpson, and going from the room, presently returned, ushering in Mr. Haldane.

CHAPTER XXXV

" MAKE yourself scarce," said Louis Redwood to Simpson, who, with a look of curiosity at his old master and a subservient lowering of eyes at his new, glided from the room. " So you've come back to the old diggings, Haldane. How long have you been here? "

" I arrived this morning," replied Mr. Haldane.

" Made your fortune, I hope."

" Hardly that, Redwood, as you can see."

There were indeed no evidences of prosperity upon him; his insolent and haughty bearing had vanished, and its place was taken by a certain humbleness of manner, in which, however, a timid rebelliousness occasionally asserted itself. That he had been on the downward course was clear enough, but there were still lower depths to reach, of which possibility he appeared to be nervously conscious.

" You don't look flourishing, I must say," observed Redwood. " Have a cigar? There's a bottle of champagne just opened. Help yourself."

Mr. Haldane did so with some show of eagerness, which was not lost upon Redwood.

" Where have you been all this time?" inquired the younger man.

" All over the world, I think," replied Mr. Haldane, " and bad luck everywhere."

" You had a good innings," said Louis Redwood, with a spice of maliciousness in his tone. " Life is a game of ups and downs."

" You've been luckier than I have been, at all events, and there's no chance of a reverse."

" I'm not sure, Haldane. So far as money goes at present, I don't dispute with you; but my turn may come next."

" You don't say that?"

" I do say it. Do you remember Lamb and Freshwater?"

" Your lawyers? Yes; I have cause to

remember them. According to what you said, they insisted upon selling me up."

" It was in their hands, you know," said Redwood carelessly, " and I had to follow their advice."

" You were rich enough to give me another lease of life," said Mr. Haldane, moodily chewing his cigar. " You told me yourself that you were not in want of money."

" I might have said something of the kind, but a bargain is a bargain. You didn't fulfil your part of it, and I didn't choose to be treated like a dog."

" What could I do? If my precious daughter would not marry you, how could I force her ? "

" You managed badly from the first. You had the game in your hands, and you threw it away. But the devil take the past! We were both well rid of each other. I should have been tired of her in a month, and she would have made me sick with her whines and tears. It made me mad to be thwarted, I own; it always does. The harder a thing is

37*

to get, the more I want it. It's my nature,
and I can't help it. You can't accuse me
of lack of perseverance. I might even have
continued with your obstinate daughter if
another woman hadn't happened to step in
my way." His face darkened. " I'm about
as successful with the second as with the first ;
and I'll know the reason why, if I'm ruined in
the end."

" Who is living at the Hall ? " asked Mr.
Haldane.

" The rooks. It has been empty ever
since the foreclosure, and Lamb & Freshwater are continually telling me it is eating
its head off. You've cost me a tidy sum one
way and another. I'm not exactly the Bank
of England, Haldane ; that is what my
lawyer friends are continually dinning into
me lately. ' You're making the pace too hot,'
they say, and when I tell them to mind their
own business they shake their heads, and
speak about pulling up and retrenching. A
pair of black ravens, that's what they are ;
but I shouldn't wonder if I had to sell Chud-

leigh, after all. I should have sold it long
ago if I could have got my price. I shall be
lucky if I see half my money back, the legal
croakers say: and what with capital lying
idle, and the loss of interest, I've no doubt
they're right. Chudleigh's gone to the dogs
since we left it. No trade, no life, no money."

" Redwood ! "

" Well ? "

" We were friends once, good friends."

" Who's disputing it ? "

"I'm down in the world. It is not my
fault, but my misfortune, that luck's gone
against me. For old times' sake don't turn
your back upon me. I'm cleaned out."

" How much will set you up ? "

" You're a good fellow, Louis. Could you
let me have a couple of hundred ? "

"It wouldn't ruin me. Look here, Haldane,
I don't set myself up as a model, and I've a
notion that I'm not exactly a favourite with
the people I mix with. Hang the lot of
them! What do I care for their opinion of
me? They'll lick my boots so long as I fling

my money about; when I'm broke they won't be able to speak bad enough of me. I know them, the curs! But there's one thing they will never be able to say, and that is that I cared for money. There's my cheque book; fill in a cheque for two hundred, and I'll sign it."

The light in Mr. Haldane's eyes as he wrote the cheque was like the light in the eyes of a condemned man who has been suddenly reprieved. He handed the pen to Redwood, who scribbled his name and threw the cheque across to the once prosperous gentleman.

"If you think of anything I can do for this, Redwood," he said and paused.

There was genuine emotion in his voice, and his hand shook as he passed it across his eyes.

"I'm not at all sure," said Redwood, "that I shan't call upon you to do something for me. You're going to Epsom to-morrow, of course?"

"I thought of going, and putting a fiver on your horse. You've backed it yourself?"

"To win a pretty large stake. What's more, I've laid against another horse in the race .that people fancy."

" I heard Morning Glory talked of."

" That is the horse I've laid against. You can go down on my drag if you like."

" I should be glad to."

" Come to breakfast here at nine. You'll find yourself in good company when we start. An old friend of yours is going with us."

" Who is he ? "

" It is a lady, hailing originally from Chudleigh."

" Not my——"

" Daughter ? O, no ; this is another kind of lady. Do you remember Honoria ? "

" Honoria ? "

" A girl from your village, a protégée of your daughter once on a time.

" I remember something of the girl."

" Did you ever hear my name mixed up with hers ? "

" Never."

" It was kept pretty close. When we first

became acquainted she knew me under another name than my own. Not an uncommon trick, Haldane. You've been on the same lay yourself. She has blossomed into a woman of fashion—but you must have heard all about it."

"You forget. I have been absent from England for some time."

"That accounts for your ignorance ; but you'll hear enough to-morrow. I'll ask you now to say good-night. Take another cigar before you go."

The old friends parted, and Mr. Haldane went away a happier man than he came.

Louis Redwood did not go to bed immediately. He took out his betting book and pencilled down how he stood on the eventful race that would be decided in a few hours. Rich as he was reputed to be the result of this race was of some importance to him. If Honoria's tip came off, Morning Glory first, and Abracadabra second, it would make a difference of a hundred and fifty thousand pounds to him. He looked rather grave as he contemplated the figures, but his confidence was not shaken. With a smile of anticipated triumph he retired to rest.

Meanwhile Mr. Haldane was undergoing an experience. Upon issuing into the street he was accosted by Simpson, who, instead of listening at keyholes, had taken it into his head to wait for his old master at the street door.

"I beg your pardon, Mr. Haldane," he said, "but I thought you might feel inclined fer a bit of a chat about old times as well as new."

To be addressed in such terms of familiarity by a man who had once been his servant was a bitter pill for Mr. Haldane to swallow, but he was accustomed to humiliation, and being in adversity a coward, he made no remonstrance.

"How has the world treated you, Simpson?"

"I can't complain," replied Simpson. "I wish it had treated you as well."

It was a feature in his offensive familiarity that he was careful not to address his old master as "sir." It was all very well in former days, but now the tables were turned, and it was principally to enjoy a practical illustration of the fact that he sought the interview.

"I am glad to hear you have prospered," said Mr. Haldane, humbly.

"Yes, I could set up as my own master now. Mr. Redwood spoke to me sharp before you, but that's his way; he hasn't much respect for anybody. I'm thinking of giving him notice."

"So well off as all that, Simpson?" said Mr. Haldane.

"I can lay my hand on three noughts, with a three before them," said Simpson, boastfully, "and then I shouldn't be broke."

"Three thousand pounds! You're a lucky man. How did you make it?"

"Honestly, and by keeping my wits about me. Mr. Redwood's horses have been a little gold mine to me."

"And to him."

"Don't be too sure of that. Taking one

year with another his stable don't cost him less than five hundred a week. He's headstrong, that's what he is. Thinks he's up to every move on the board, thinks he's a match for jockeys and trainers, thinks he's a match for women, while, if the truth was known, he's made to pay all round by the whole lot of them. He's got a certainty to-morrow though. The Derby's as good as won. Put a bit on Abracadabra, Mr. Haldane."

"Thank you, Simpson."

"It's a pity about Chudleigh, isn't it, Mr. Haldane?"

"Mr. Redwood tells me it is in a bad way."

"Gone to the dogs. You'd hardly know the old place."

"They'd be glad to have me back again, Simpson."

"They'd be glad to have anybody back again. Have you seen your daughter?"

"No."

"She lives in lodgings, No. 5, Pole Street, Buckingham Palace Road. It is a come-down, isn't it, for all of you? Well, I must wish you ta-ta; I've got to be up early in the morning. I thought it wouldn't look friendly to let you go without having a word with you."

He held out his hand, which Mr. Haldane pretended not to see.

"Good-night, Simpson," he said, and walked away.

"Proud beast!" muttered Simpson, looking after him. "Wouldn't shake hands with me, wouldn't he? But I showed him I was as good as he was. I'm glad he's come down."

He went up to his room, and before he sought his bed devoted quite an hour to seeking inspirations for the Derby. He wrote on separate pieces of paper the names of all the horses that were being backed for the race, and shaking them up in a hat, drew one forth. Opening the paper he had drawn he read the name on it, "Morning Glory." He smiled, folded the paper, and put it back in the hat, and then began shaking all the pieces out of it till only one remained. Opening it, he read again, "Morning Glory." His second smile was not quite so confident as his first, but his faith in Abracadabra still remained firm. He took up a book from the table, and opened it hap-hazard. The first letter on the top of the page was M for Morning. He opened another page hap-hazard, and the first letter was G for Glory. He was manifestly disturbed by these occult prognostications, and he began to question whether Abracadabra was really the certainty for the Derby it was pronounced to be. Every description of sporting paper was in the room ; he consulted them all. Without a single exception every sporting prophet gave Abracadabra as the winner. He became reassured ; it was not possible they could all be mistaken. As a two-year-old Abracadabra had won three races, and this year had been favourite for the Two Thousand, which he won, as he had his other races, with the greatest ease. In his preparation for the Derby there had not been a hitch, not a mishap, not one day's sickness, and it was a well-known fact that the whole stable to a man was on the favourite. Simpson smiled

again with returned confidence, and examined
his betting book. Yes, he stood to win five
hundred pounds, or lose two hundred, on
Abracadabra. During his service with Louis
Redwood he had become quite a man of the
town, and as he often declared, was up to
every move on the board ; therefore he kept
his bets duly recorded in a regular betting
book, after the fashion of his superiors. He
was not high enough in social station to be a
member of Tattersall's or even of the Vic-
toria ; but he belonged to the Beaufort, and,
as an ambitious man, looked forward to ad-
vancement. He was intimate with many of
the racing fraternity, and knew that every
one of them who had made money had risen
from nothing. There were some who could
hardly write their names in their cheque
books, but they had amazing heads for
figures, and as for their histories before they
were in a position to drive blood horses and
wear huge diamond rings and pins, the least
said about them the better. The men upon
whose downfall they had fattened were mem-

bers of old families with old estates which
had passed from them, and of new families
created by prosperous tradesmen and specu-
lators whose lives had been devoted to the
making of fortunes which their children were
squandering. Simpson had made the acquaintance of numbers of these rooks and
pigeons, and by dint of natural shrewdness
and cunning had managed to pick up a good
many stray crumbs which had swelled his
banking account to its present respectable
figure. But why should he stop at three
thousand pounds? Here in his master's horse
was his opportunity; it was the chance of a
lifetime, and might never occur again. Why
should he not turn bookmaker, and, as well
as backing Abracadabra, lay against all the
other horses in the race? He had often
thought of turning bookmaker on his own
account, and this Derby, which was " all
over but the shouting," would be a capital
commencement. With fair luck his three
thousand would be thirty before the racing
season was over. Debating this question with

doubts and fears, now being urged on by the
one, now being pulled back by the other, he
once more tossed all the pieces of paper
together, and drew one out. The last time
he did so was with his right hand and his
eyes open. This time he closed his eyes and
drew with his left hand. Again, " Morning
Glory ! " What did it mean ? Was it Fate
that was whispering to him not to turn bookmaker yet, but to desert Abracadabra, and
take the odds to a large amount against
Morning Glory ? He would try again —
hanged if he wouldn't. He smoothed one of
the sporting papers in which all the probable
starters for the Derby and their jockeys were
set down. Then he took a pin, and with
averted eyes stuck it in the list. With
feverish eagerness he looked at the paper ;
the pin was sticking in " Morning Glory."
He stood for a long time glaring at it ; then
he tumbled into bed very much disturbed in
his mind. The chances of Abracadabra
winning the great race were not half so good
as they had been an hour ago.

CHAPTER XXXVI.

THIS Derby day was not different from all other Derby days. There were the same tumult and hurly-burly; the same vast gathering of people of all degrees and conditions in life, peers, statesmen, costermongers, layers and backers of horses, acrobats, tipsters, ladies, courtezans, gipsies, and general hangers-on : the same contrasts of wealth and poverty, of hope and despair, of false hilarity and blank misery. Nature alone made genuine holiday ; the sun shone brightly, and touched the surrounding hills and gay dresses of the ladies with shifting light. In its colour, animation, variety, and significance, the scene at Epsom on a Derby day is incomparable.

Of all the motley gathering not one

attracted more attention than Honoria. The admiration was bestowed in some quarters openly, in others covertly and envyingly. Men pointed her out to each other, and ladies levelled their opera glasses at her. She was conscious of this general attention, but did not show it. The absence of small vanity in this beautiful creature was as remarkable as her possession of absolutely high qualities which, if scandal had not been busy with her name, would have entitled her to the homage which, openly by some and grudgingly by others, was paid to her. She had driven down to Epsom with Louis Redwood's party, and she wore the mixed colours of Abra-cadabra and Morning Glory. Redwood would have protested against this divided allegiance if he dared, but the power she wielded over him was due as much to her courage and independence as to her beauty, and he knew it was wiser to be silent on certain matters upon which they differed. When she was not occupied in the paddock and with persons who were executing com-

missions for her, she held court in her box,
bestowing her smiles and favour upon those
who thronged around her, in a queenly
fashion which strengthened her hold upon
them. Mr. Haldane had been introduced to
her, and from the moment he saw her his
eyes seldom wandered from her when they
were near each other. She had awakened
within him a memory of the past. The
queenly woman reminded him strangely of a
woman whom he had betrayed and deserted.
Memories also were awakened within Honoria
upon Redwood's mention of his name. Since
the night upon which she had travelled from
Chudleigh to London in the company of Mr.
Millington she had not seen or heard from
Miss Haldane. She had, as we know, written
a letter to her benefactor, to the lady who
had saved her probably from death, certainly
from despair, warning her of the character of
the man who was wooing her; that done,
all was at an end between them. She had
thought often of the lady who had played the
part of an angel in her life of poverty and

38*

early shame, but when she became notorious she did not deem herself worthy to approach her in any way. On one side were virtue and purity, on the other, vice and degradation; she acknowledged the position, and cut herself aloof from one with whom she was not fit to associate. She gazed with curiosity upon Mr. Haldane when he was introduced to her, and noted wonderingly his strange observance of her, in which there was a touch of subserviency. In Chudleigh village he had never bestowed the least attention upon her, and she did not remember that he had ever addressed her. On the road a somewhat significant conversation had taken place between them.

" You have been absent from England for some time," she said.

" Yes," he replied, " for some time."

" Since your return," she continued, " have you been down to Chudleigh ? "

" No ; I only returned yesterday."

" I am wondering whether it is much altered."

" Mr. Redwood tells me that a great change has come over the place."

" That would be the case, of course, the Hall being empty. It is sad to lose so fine a place."

" I have felt it deeply."

" Mr. Haldane, have you no remembrance of me ? " She noticed again the strange look in his eyes.

" You remind me of someone," he said, with hesitancy.

" Of myself," she said, smiling.

" No ; not of yourself. May I ask how old you are ? "

" Some ladies would be angry with you. I am twenty-three. You ought to remember me, Mr. Haldane. I am almost a Chudleigh girl. Your daughter was very kind to me."

He winced at the reference to his daughter.

" I hope she is well."

" I do not know; I have not seen her lately."

" Are you not friendly with her ? "

" She disobeyed me."

Honoria was but imperfectly acquainted with the details of the relations between him and Louis Redwood, but her natural intelligence enabled her to arrive immediately at a correct conclusion.

" You wished her to marry," she said.

" It is a subject," he said, " I would rather avoid."

" I am very self-willed, Mr. Haldane. You wished her to marry Mr. Redwood ? "

" It would have been the saving of me, and the making of her."

" What are you two talking about so softly and mysteriously ? " cried Redwood, turning towards them

" Family matters," said Honoria dryly. "Do not interrupt us."

" Be careful of her, Haldane," said Redwood. " She is a witch."

" I will make a confession to you," she said, addressing herself again to Mr. Haldane, " though it is hardly that, for I never disguise from myself or from others, what I am. You know the world's opinion of me."

"Oh, the world!" he exclaimed, with an awkward movement of his hands expressing at once that the world's opinion was not worth considering, and that he would rather not be pressed to give his own.

"Yes, the world," she said; "but it is curious, now, that it is only half right. What do you think yourself of the intimacy between me and Mr. Redwood? You hesitate to answer, but your very hesitation is in itself the answer; and yet you are about as right as the world is. Upon the virtues of Mr. Redwood you, who have known him so long and so well, must have a very exact estimate. Answer me candidly. Would he have been a fit husband for your daughter?"

"I cannot discuss the question," he said. He was beginning to be afraid of this outspoken creature.

"It is not a subject for discussion," she said, "because there can be but one opinion. Mr. Redwood would have ruined her happiness and her life, and it is well for her that she did not give him the chance. Why, if he offered to marry me I would laugh in his face."

"Still plotting?" said Redwood.

"Running you down, Redwood," said Honoria. "Taking your character away. I am tearing you to pieces; Mr. Haldane is defending you. Which side will you bet on?"

"Yours; and Haldane, if he is wise, will agree in everything you say."

"I am trying to bring him round. So," to Mr. Haldane, "you see you were wrong."

"Right or wrong," he said, moodily, "it is all over now. You have asked me a good many questions; I should like to ask you one." She nodded assent. "You say you are almost a Chudleigh girl. Do your people live there?"

"My people! What do you mean by that?"

"Your parents, your relations?"

"I have neither parents nor relations. Would you believe, Mr. Haldane, that you are talking to a human being who has not a single tie in the whole wide world?"

"I believe whatever you say."

"That is polite of you. It is a fact. To my knowledge, there is not a man, woman, or child with whom I can claim kindred. I must bring something to your mind. In the village of Bittern, seven or eight miles from Chudleigh, there lived a woman with a little child. I am not telling you a fairy story, and I shall not treat you to a mystery. The child was myself. I can just remember the woman, of whom I know nothing more than that she was not my mother. How it came about that at the age of six or seven I found myself quite alone in the world I cannot say, but it is true. In the first place, I was deserted by my parents, whoever they may be; in the second place, I was deserted by the woman who, for some reason or other, had looked after me for a time. Imagine, if you please, a young child thrown by human cruelty into such a position. There is a kind of brutality in it, is there not? How I managed to live is really inexplicable. Then came a day I remember well. I was sitting

by a hedge on the roadside, shivering and
hungry and in rags, when a carriage came
along. In the carriage was a little girl about
as old as myself, who was taking a ride with
her nurse. This little girl insists upon
getting out of the carriage, and she speaks to
me, and actually gives me some sweets; and
insists, too, upon taking me back with her to
Chudleigh. There are some memories that
never fade, and this is one. My benefactor,
Mr. Haldane, was your daughter."

"I have a recollection of the circumstance," he said. He would have preferred
to be silent, the last of his wishes being to
encourage a conversation into which his
daughter was introduced, but Honoria had
paused and looked at him, expecting him to
speak.

"Her kindness," continued Honoria, "did
not end there. She took the charge of me
upon herself, and paid a woman in Chudleigh
for my keep. She was the means, also, of
my receiving a better education than was
bestowed upon the regular village children,

and so, Mr. Haldane, I grew into quite a superior young woman. How I grew into what I am is my affair, and proves my ingratitude to your daughter. I owe her a debt I can never repay, and with all my heart and soul I thank God that you did not succeed in forcing her into a marriage with Mr. Redwood. It comes into my mind, Mr. Haldane, that I am indebted to you."

" In what way ?" he asked.

" Your daughter must have thrown away a good deal of money upon me, which, of course, you must have given her."

" She had her allowance," said Mr. Haldane, " and could do what she liked with it."

" Am I right in supposing that you are in rather low water just now ? "

" I have had a run of bad luck," he said. There was no refinement or delicacy in his nature ; he was ready to accept anything from her.

" Consider me in your debt to the tune of —how much shall we say ? Five hundred pounds ?"

"You are too good," he said, with a beating heart.

"Not at all. Indirectly I am your debtor, and I can spare a good deal more than that. I will not give you the money now, because it might be noticed. On the course, when nobody is looking. I have brought a large sum with me, to do some ready money betting with. Then, so far as you are concerned, we are quits. There—we will talk no more about it. Only take my tip. Back Morning Glory."

"Really?"

"Really. I am in luck just now. Everything I touch turns to gold."

It seemed so. On the first race, the Chetwynd Plate, she netted a thousand pounds, and Mr. Haldane and Major Causton, taking her tip, each won a fair stake. Redwood lost as much as Honoria won. It needed only that Honoria should say that Prince of Tyre would win to cause him to back the two second favourites, Red Cherry and Saint. He would prove to her that she was no match for him in such matters; he would show that he was her master, and that she was playing a game in which she was a novice. Therefore he made a plunge on his fancies, and backed his two horses against her one at even money for a monkey.

"Blind luck!" he muttered, as Prince of Tyre came in first by two lengths. "But she shall suffer for it on the Derby."

Honoria smiled calmly on him when the winning number went up.

"You don't believe in luck, Redwood," she said.

" Luck be hanged!" he cried. "Wait for the Derby,"

The Derby was the next race, and the course and everybody on it, with the exception of Honoria, was in a state of the greatest excitement. The yelling and shrieking, the shouting of odds, the rushing to and fro, the white faces, the mad throbbing of hopes and fears, converted the lovely spot into a pandemonium. The party in whom we are most interested went into the paddock to see the horses saddled.   They were all in the pink of condition, fit to run for a man's life, and seemed to be aware that they were about to engage in the most important contest of the year.   Before Abracadabra's jockey, the celebrated Beane, was weighed in, Redwood drew him aside.   No one intruded upon them, but curious eyes watched them and sought to glean information from signs.

"What do you think, Beane?" asked Redwood.

"What everybody thinks, sir," replied the jockey.   "I don't believe the horse can lose."

He looked at his employer in expectancy; Redwood chewed his moustache.

"You are on," he said, "two thousand to nothing."

Beane elevated his forefinger, and a satisfied expression appeared on his face.

"It's a certainty, sir; you can back Abracadabra for all you're worth."

There was another little confidential and anxious conversation between Redwood and the trainer, the result of which was perfectly satisfactory to the owner. He beckoned one of the commissioners in his employ, and in less than five minutes it was known that he had thrown another heavy commission in the market, and had backed Abracadabra to win a further fifty thousand pounds. The effect of this was to considerably shorten the odds. "I'll take five to four," shrieked the bookmakers. "Fives, bar one." Before you could turn round the betting on Abracadabra was six to four on, and the odds against Morning Glory had lengthened to six to one. Some of the leading bookmakers refused to take the odds on the favourite, and the consequence was that Abracadabra's admirers in many instances had to lay seven to four and two to one. Honoria called Major Causton to her side.

"Get the longest odds you can," she said, "against Morning Glory for a thousand. Come back to me immediately."

Redwood, hearing this, exclaimed, " Are you mad?"

" Wait a moment, Redwood," she replied,

smiling at him, and she turned aside with Mr.
Haldane. " What do you want to say? "

" They tell me it's throwing money away to
back anything but the favourite."

" Do as you please with your money," said
Honoria; she had given him five hundred
pounds, and the money he had won on the
Chetwynd Plate burned in his pocket. He
had to bet with ready money bookmakers; it
was known he had come down in the world.
" What difference can it make to me whether
you win or lose? "

" If you are fool enough to back Morning
Glory," said Redwood, intercepting him as
he left Honoria, " you deserve to lose every
penny you have got. She has been telling you
to back the horse, hasn't she? Out with it! "

" Yes, she told me to back it."

" What the devil does she know about
horses? " cried Redwood. " Look here,
Haldane. Have women ever brought you
any luck ? "

" They have been my destruction," muttered Mr. Haldane.

"Well, then. Follow Honoria, and find yourself in the gutter. Don't come to me to help you out of it."

Mr. Haldane walked away in an agony of doubt; he did not know what to do.

"Now, Redwood," said Honoria, "you want to know if I am mad. Upon my word, I half believe I am; I've got Morning Glory on the brain. It's on the cards that my fancy will beggar me."

"With all my heart," he said, "I hope it will." And thought, "If I could bring that about she would be at my mercy. It is only because she is independent of me that she is torturing me so. If I could beggar her! If I could beggar her!"

"You are thinking of something wicked," she said, tapping her foot with her sunshade. "Am I looking well to-day?"

"You are a beautiful devil," he replied, "and I would give all I'm worth to tame you."

"I dare say you would," she said, with a saucy smile. "We are having a rare fight,

you and I. The question is, who will be
victor in the end ? "

" You'll be eating humble pie, my lady,
before the day is over."

" That's to be seen. You ought to know
by this time how obstinate a woman can be.
I have a notion, Redwood, that I can read
your thoughts. Shall I try ? "

" Yes."

" Well, you are thinking that it would
better your chances if you could ruin me."

" You are a witch."

" I offer you the opportunity. I throw
down my glove. If you are anything of a
man you will pick it up. I dare you ! "

She flashed a look into his eyes that almost
electrified him.

" I pick up your glove," he said. " What
is the challenge ? "

CHAPTER XXXVII

THE RACE.

HONORIA looked around. Although there were numbers of people in the paddock they were all so engrossed in their own selfish affairs that they had no time to notice that she and Louis Redwood were engaged in an unusually animated conversation. A certain measure of privacy was therefore secured, but it did not content Honoria. She made a slight motion of her head, and Redwood followed her as a lamb follows it dam. She conducted him to a remote corner, where there was no chance of their being hustled or overheard.

"Redwood," she said, "do you know I have a great deal of money?"

"You ought to have," he replied. "You have been a regularly lucky woman this last year. You never back a loser. Boats, dogs,

39*

or horses, it's all one to you; whatever you put your money on, wins. Your luck has been dead in; but mark my words, Honoria, the Derby turns it. I wish you had every penny you're worth on Morning Glory."

"I am game to risk it," she said. "That is my challenge. Morning Glory against Abracadabra for every shilling I possess."

"You've got a nerve," he said admiringly; "but it's two to one on Abracadabra, and five or six to one against Morning Glory. If you lost thirty thousand could you stump up?"

"I could."

"And you want me to lay you the odds against Morning Glory. Well, to be honest with you, Honoria, if by some infernal chance you should win I shouldn't be able to raise money enough to settle with you. As for getting such a sum on in the ring at this time of the day it would be an impossibility."

"I don't want money, Redwood," said Honoria, with a bewitching smile, "I want landed property."

" Landed property ? "

" Landed property," she repeated. " Women take odd notions into their heads; I've taken one into mine. What has the Chudleigh estate cost you ? "

" Cost me ! " he cried with an oath. " I'd rather not mention the sum. It makes me wild to think of it."

" I challenge you," said she, tauntingly, " to lay me the deeds of the Chudleigh estate against thirty thousand pounds of my money that Morning Glory does not win the Derby."

He stared at her in blank amazement. " Are you mad ? " he exclaimed.

" I think I am. You haven't the pluck ! Good-bye, then." She turned, as though throwing him over for ever.

" Not so fast, my lady," he said, with white lips. " No one has ever seen me show the white feather yet where money is concerned. I was thinking more of you than of myself."

" I've no objection to your thinking of me," she said, firing him with another look and a charming smile. "I do believe you mean it when you say you love me."

"You may believe it. I would sell my soul for you."

"It hasn't a market value, Redwood; Chudleigh has; and mad as I am on this fancy of mine, I'm a business woman. Do you really and truly love me, Louis?"

He thrilled with pleasure as she addressed him by his Christian name. "Haven't I done enough to prove it, Honoria?"

"Not quite enough," she replied.

"By ——!" he swore another oath to emphasise his words. "Here have I been hanging about you ever since you have been in London, adoring you, worshipping you, gratifying every wish, drawing cheques, buying diamonds—Oh, I'm not throwing it in your teeth, my lady; I'm only going through the catalogue—waiting on you hand and foot, making myself a perfect slave, and all I've got for it is a kiss of your hand——"

"When you wanted my lips," she interrupted saucily.

She had never looked more lovely; she knew her power, and was exercising it.

"I want *you!*" he cried, hoarse with passion.

"Who knows what may happen," she asked saucily, "when I really need a friend like you—when I am ruined? As I shall be if you accept my challenge, and your horse wins the Derby. You could make your own terms. Do you dare?"

"Do I dare?" he retorted scornfully. "The challenge is made."

"Let us enter it," she said, and she made an entry in her dainty betting book, he doing the same in his. "Is this right, Louis?" She held out her book to him.

"Quite right," he replied.

"You may as well initial it," she said, "and I will initial yours."

The interchange was made, and then they shook hands, both smiling into each other's eyes, confident of victory.

The paddock was emptying now; all the jockeys had passed the scales, and some

were already mounted and making their way
to the course; the others were mounting and
accompanied by anxious trainers, owners, and
backers, were following the leaders; the bookmakers' touts, having nothing more to pick
up in that arena, were in the ring. Honoria
and Redwood walked slowly to their box,
both apparently cool and unconcerned; they
had made the great stake, of which no one
was at present aware but themselves, and it
was one of Redwood's boasts that he could
lose and win a hundred thousand pounds
without turning a hair. Nevertheless, although
he was completely successful in concealing his
feelings, he was inwardly much agitated. So
much depended upon the next half-hour! His
life's triumph or defeat seemed to hang upon
the issue.

"By Jove, you two!" cried Major Causton.
"One would think you hadn't a penny on the
race. Let me congratulate you beforehand,
Redwood. There's no getting a bookmaker
to take another fiver against Abracadabra.
There he goes. What a beauty!"

The horses were cantering to the starting-post, and every eye was noting Abracadabra, and every voice was raised in admiration. A trainer whispered a word to Redwood.

" Declined," he said aloud.

" Sixteen thousand," said the trainer.

" Thanks," drawled Redwood, taking out a cigar. " Not for double the money."

" What is it, Redwood ? " inquired Honoria.

" An offer of sixteen thousand for Abra-cadabra," replied Redwood, " if he wins."

" He will be worth nearly as much," said Honoria, " if he comes in second by a head."

" Why of course," Major Causton put in, " in that case the horse is yours. Eh, Redwood ? "

" That's so," said Redwood. " I hope my head won't ache till then."

Two or three asked the meaning of this, and Redwood himself explained it. When it became known that Honoria had such faith in Morning Glory some anxious souls rushed off to back it. These were men who believed in following the luck, and who were aware that Honoria had been having a wonderful run of late.

"They'll not thank you presently," said Redwood, looking after them savagely.

"Redwood and I are having a battle royal," remarked Honoria to Major Causton. "He swears by Abracadabra, I by Morning Glory. We have just made a heavy bet on our fancies."

"That's no one's affair but our own," said Redwood, in surprise.

"I don't know about that," rejoined Honoria, looking through her glasses at the horses going to the post. "Such a bet as we have just made is sure to leak out. There's no keeping a thing secret in these days, is there, Major?"

"It's difficult," said Causton, "if not impossible, with all these gadflies buzzing around. So you've turned bookmaker, Redwood."

"It is a whim of hers," replied Redwood.

"She threw out a challenge, and I accepted it."

"If I lose," said Honoria, "I |shall be ruined."

"What!" cried the Major. "You are joking."

"Not much of a joke," observed Honoria, "to lose thirty thousand pounds in one fell swoop. That is the correct quotation, I believe."

Major Causton's eyes travelled from her to Redwood, and back again. "You're a pair of bantams. What odds have you got?"

"Landed estate," said Honoria quietly. "When I see Morning Glory's number the first to go up I shall be the mistress of Chudleigh. I refer you to Redwood."

"There's no trusting to a woman's tongue," said Redwood, sulkily. "It's a true bill. And when she sees Abracadabra's number go up first she'll be the poorer by thirty thousand pounds."

Major Causton whistled.

"Then," said Honoria, in her sweetest

voice, "I shall have to commence life all over again, and Redwood has promised to be my friend."

"I understand," said Causton. "It's one throw of the dice, and the battle's lost or won. Lady of Chudleigh, or——"

She finished the sentence for him. "Or a poor girl without a frock to her back, as I was when Redwood first knew me."

No further words were exchanged; all their attention was now centred on the horses, which had reached the post. It was not an easy job for the starter; again and again the line was broken before he lowered his flag.

"What's that devil breaking away?" shouted a man in the rear who had no glasses to assist him.

No one near him replied; it was Abracadabra. In this particular box the onlooker's were too deeply absorbed by conflicting passion to speak. From the near distance below them in the ring came the answer:

"It's the favourite! I'll take seven to four in hundreds."

"Done!" cried a backer, and the bet was booked.

A sigh of relief escasped from hundreds of the spectators who had backed Abracadabra; the horse had only gone fifty yards, and was now leisurely turning round. Louis Redwood never took his eyes from his Voightlander. A loud shout arose from the vast throng. "They're off! They're off!" And a moment afterwards. "No! False start!" Abracadabra was the last to pull up.

Major Causton glanced at Redwood, but could read nothing on that gentleman's face. Had Redwood's thoughts been expressed in words he would have heard "Damn him! What is he up to?" But such outspoken utterance would have been considered bad form. In these preliminary movements Morning Glory had behaved admirably, showing not the least symptom of fretfulness or nervousness. The betting on the race was for the most part over; only here and there did a small ready-money bookmaker or a welsher give occasional odds. Once more the horses seemed to be getting fairly in line, and again Abracadabra broke away; and still Redwood's face exhibited no trace of emotion. There was a delay of a couple of minutes, during which Redwood calmly wiped the film from his glass.

"He takes it coolly," thought Major Causton. "I should be another Vesuvius if I were in his place. Is there anything wrong with Abracadabra?"

There had now been three false starts, and the suspense to many was maddening. For the fourth time a mighty roar rang out, "They're off! They're off!" The two white flags were dropped, one after another, and the bell was rung. A sudden hush fell upon the assembled thousands, each interested spectator following the movements of his own horse with suppressed excitement. Presently, however, tongues became loosened, and remarks were made and questions asked as the horses changed positions. Abracadabra

and Morning Glory had both got well off, and
were lying sixth and seventh, Morning Glory
being at the favourite's heels. So they ran
for three quarters of a mile. Redwood was
quite satisfied with the position of his horse,
whose jockey was following out his instruc-
tions to the letter, but occupied as he was in
watching Abracadabra he cast an uneasy
glance now and again at Morning Glory,
whose tactics seemed to be to wait upon the
favourite about three-quarters of a length in
the rear. That Morning Glory should keep
this unvarying position till they reached
Tattenham Corner was a torment to Redwood,
who would have been better pleased to see the
horse he feared fall a length or two behind,
or even to forge ahead before the real pinch
came. The voices of the spectators grew
louder as the horses rounded Tattenham
Corner. The pace had been a cracker from
the start, and now the leaders, having shot
their bolt, lost ground at every stride. Up
the straight they came, a gaily-coloured
cavalcade of joy and misery. Abracadabra

and Morning Glory were now fourth and
fifth, their relative positions being precisely
the same as they had been all through the
race. The air was pierced with shouts, and
screams, and yells. "Ten to one on the
favourite! Abracadabra wins! The favourite
wins! What about Morning Glory?" They
were second and third now; the leader, an
outsider succumbed, and they were first and
second, and within two hundred yards of the
winning post. A chill fell upon Louis Redwood even in the midst of his excitement.
It seemed to him as if Morning Glory had not
varied an inch in its position towards Abracadabra, and as if Fate were waiting the final
flash of a moment to deal him a fatal blow.
Nothing else was in the race but these two
horses, their nearest competitor being three
lengths behind. A hundred yards only to the
winning post, and Morning Glory drew slowly
up. "Abracadabra wins! The favourite
wins! The favourite! The favourite! Morning Glory! I'll take two to one Morning
Glory! Morning Glory! Morning Glory!

Abracadabra!" The din was deafening; it was as if Babel had broke loose. Hearts beat almost to bursting, faces flushed, eyes glared, voices were strained till they were in danger of cracking. A man fell down in a fit, foaming at the mouth, but no one paid him any attention. By a stroke of masterly riding Morning Glory's jockey had stolen in between Abracadabra and the rails; Beane had no need to turn his head; he felt the snort of his rival's nostrils; only four strides and the goal was reached. At the first of these four strides Morning Glory was within half a head of Abracadabra; at the second within a quarter of a head; at the third they were neck and neck. Fortune, fame, reputation, years of pleasure, the degradation of lives, rescue from despair and shame, hung upon the last stride of these noble animals, whose jockeys, at the supreme moment seemed to lift them to the winning post, which they passed amidst a scene of indiscribable excitement.

"The favourite's won! No, Morning Glory!

I'll take odds it's a dead heat! Yes, a dead heat—a dead heat!"

A shrewd, mottle-faced bookmaker leaning against a post made his deep voice heard through all the uproar.

"Two monkeys to one on Morning Glory!"

Redwood heard and recognised this voice, and he knew that when the issue of a race was in doubt it never erred. He did not move however; his eyes were fixed upon the board. Scarcely two or three moments had elapsed since the horses had passed the post, but it seemed an age. The men were waiting on the platform with numbers in their hands, looking towards the judge's box for their instruction. They stooped, and selected a number, and before they fixed it in its place the result was yelled all over the course. The number was 2. Morning Glory was declared the winner. Abracadabra second.

With a smile on his lips and a curse in his heart, Louis Redwood dropped his glass, and as he put it in its sling he turned to Honoria.

"You have won," he said.

Honoria nodded, and returned his smile.

She was a little dazed, because she did not yet quite realize the situation, but she betrayed very little excitement. In the first flush of his defeat Louis Redwood gave scarcely a thought to the material stake he had lost. It was the probable loss of Honoria that stung him most; she had slipped from his grasp in the very moment of his triumph, and still remained her own mistress, more than ever independent of him. There was yet a hope, however—a slender one, it is true, but it had happened before, and might happen now—that the winning jockey could not draw the weight. He offered his arm to Honoria.

"Coming to the paddock?" he asked.

"Yes," she replied, and placing her hand on his arm walked with him. She could not but admire him for his ease and self-possession. "Are you going to raise an objection?" she inquired.

"Objection be hanged!" he exclaimed. "The race is fairly won and lost. How do you feel?"

40*

" I don't know yet; I'll tell you by and by. How do *you* feel after such a knock?"

" Oh, it isn't the money that troubles me," he said. " It's you. Are we friends still?"

" Why, certainly. What should I do without you?"

There was comfort in this. " You've said it, mind," he cried.

" I've said it," she replied. " It will depend upon yourself."

" In what way?"

" Didn't I tell you I don't know yet? I must have time to get my breath. I've a great deal to think of now. Hunted out of Chudleigh the last time I was there. Returning to it its mistress and lady. There, don't let's talk about it just now. The mere thought of it bewilders me."

" Only one question. Am I invited to the house-warming?"

" Of course you are. The house-warming! Yes, I dare say I shall give you one. It will be rare fun. You're first on the list."

They met the returning horses at the gate of the paddock. As Morning Glory came in first between the divided line of spectators the jockey and Honoria exchanged a smiling glance.

" Hallo ! " whispered Redwood to her.

" O, yes," said Honoria, as if answering a question. " We have understood each other for weeks past. We each played our own bats, Redwood."

" Where did you get your brains from ? " he asked.

" That's the question. I'm a waif and stray, you know."

" You're the loveliest woman in England."

" Especially now," she said, showing her white teeth.

" Especially always," he retorted. " I have never wavered."

" You forget. You did once."

" That belongs to ancient history."

" It was only yesterday. I can see myself at this moment in Chudleigh Woods. Good God ! I was going to throw myself into the lake! And now!"—she could not finish the sentence.

The jockeys passed the scales, and the voices of the racing touts rang through the air. "All right!" "All right!" Redwood did not exchange a word with his jockey Beane; he believed in his heart that he had been sold.

His disasters did not end here; the day was not yet over. He and Honoria had heavy bets on the next two races, the High Weight Handicap and the Stanley Stakes, and the result was the same. He lost, and Honoria won.

"Your star is in the ascendant." he said.

"I hear you have a notion of giving a house-warming at Chudleigh," said Major Causton to her. " Is the furniture at the Hall yours as well as the estate?"

"I never thought of that," she replied, and at once attacked Redwood.

"I will make you a present of it," he said grandly.

"It is not mine, then?" she asked.

" You did not win it," he said. What you won was landed property. I should like to lay you under an obligation to me."

" I am under too many already. Besides, I don't wish to bleed you to death."

" What does it matter ? " he muttered.

" Oh, I have a heart, though you may not believe it. No, I will not accept the gift. What do you value the lot at, pictures, furniture, belongings, everything ? "

" I am no tradesman."

" But name a sum—a fancy sum, if you like."

" Say five thousand pounds ; but I don't sell."

" We'll bet on it."

" Anything you like."

The numbers for the next race, the Juvenile Plate, were going up.

" Let us try our luck," she suggested. " I'll take odds against evens, and bet you five thousand pounds to everything that is in the Hall."

" I'm content," said Redwood, and the bet was made.

The race was run, and up went the No. 7.

Redwood laughed, and said, "Nicked again. Now you are mistress of everything. If you want a waiter, hire me."

"Upon my soul," said one of the party. "She can't lose. Providence is on her side."

"I believe in the other gentleman," observed Redwood. "This is a black Wednesday for me, and no mistake."

CHAPTER XXXVIII.

IT is time to turn our attention to the other side of the picture and it will be a relief to many to leave the seamy side of human nature awhile.

From the day Agnes Haldane left her father's house she had led a life of patient toil. She and Rachel Diprose did not remain long in the lodgings they took when they first came to London ; at Mr. Palmer's wish Agnes took rooms close to his residence in Westminster Palace road, and thus she had a friend near her upon whom she could rely. His first anxiety was, how they should live ? She and Rachel, as we know, had but little money between them, and they set to work at once to solve the problem upon which hundreds of thousands of people in this great

city are engaged from the cradle to the grave.
Agnes and her faithful maid had many a
battle with respect to expenditure. The
young lady did not wish to touch Rachel's
store, but George Millington's sweetheart
would not be denied.

" Bless you, my dear young lady," said
Rachel, "what you've got won't keep you a
month, and then what are you going to do?
If you don't use my money I'll throw it in
the fire, and then, if you please, you won't be
hard enough to turn me away to starve.
For that's what it will come to. And even
then I'll never leave you. You can call in
the police, of course, but I don't think
they'll take me up, because you won't be
table to make them believe I'm doing anything wrong."

" But, dear Rachel," urged Agnes, "can't
you see the difficulty you're placing me in ? "

" No, Miss, I can't," said Rachel stoutly,
" and that's flat."

" I insist upon your listening to reason,
Rachel."

" I'll listen to anything you say, Miss, but that doesn't mean that I shall agree with it."

" Sit down, and hear reason." Rachel sat down and gazed stolidly before her. "Look at me, Rachel."

"Yes, Miss; but don't break my heart, please."

" You foolish girl, you know I love you too well for that."

" And I love you too well, Miss, if you'll forgive me for saying so, to leave you all alone in this great black city, with its crowds of strangers, and its smoke, and its hard ways."

" I know you love me, Rachel, but you must remember your duty."

" It's what I am remembering, Miss."

" I shall be cross with you if you interrupt me, Rachel."

" Then I won't speak another word, Miss," and Rachel threw her apron over her face.

Agnes softly removed it, and her fingers touched Rachel's neck caressingly. Rachel caught her young lady's hand, and kissed it

and would not let it go. It was only by
the exercise of gentle force tnat Agnes could
release herself, for it was manifestly impossible
for her to say what was in her mind with the
faithful girl hanging on to her hand like that.

"I'm afraid," said Agnes, reprovingly,
"that you are very backward in some things."

"Begging your pardon, Miss," said Rachel,
boldly, " so are you."

"Tell me my faults, Rachel."

Only too glad for this diversion, Rachel
said : "Well, Miss, in cooking, for one
thing."

"I fear you are right, Rachel, but I shall
soon learn."

"Pray, Miss, who are you going to learn
from ?"

"Oh, I shall teach myself," replied Agnes,
feeling herself at a disadvantage.

"It's not possible, Miss.   You couldn't
learn a foreign language without a book, or
a guide, or living in a foreign country.   Now,
could you, Miss ?"

"It would be difficult, I own," said Agnes,

who could not resist a smile at this direct thrust.

"That's where it is, Miss.   Cooking's a foreign language to you."

"No, Rachel, it is a very different thing."

"Why, how can you say so, Miss?   When I was out yesterday, didn't you try to boil a potatoe?   What came of it?"

"Not a boiled potatoe, certainly," confessed Agnes, laughing outright.

"That settles it, Miss," said Rachel, and would have risen from her chair if Agnes had not forced her down.

"It does not settle it.   I shall learn in a little while."

"Three times have you tried, Miss," said the obstinate Rachel, "and three times have you made a—well, I won't say what of it. It'll take you years to learn, and do you think I could sit by, and never see a floury one on your plate?   No, I couldn't.   I should be a murderer."

"A murderer, Rachel!   Oh, you foolish girl!"

"Not at all, Miss. To eat 'em as you boil 'em would be the death of you, and it's me that would bring it about."

"Is there any arguing with such a creature?" asked Agnes, casting bright looks around.

"No, Miss, there isn't." And Rachel tried to rise again, as though the discussion had reached its natural end.

"You will make me angry with you, Rachel."

"Anything but that, Miss," said Rachel, with a deep sigh of resignation, "except leaving you.'

"Rachel, my dear, you have a sweet-heart?"

"I have, Miss; as good a man as ever stepped."

"He loves you fondly, you fortunate girl, and you must do your duty by him."

"I'm doing it, Miss, by keeping with you."

"Now, Rachel, Rachel!"

"It's true, Miss. If he thought different I'd never look at him again, because neither my George nor any man shall ever make me do what I think is wrong."

"Is it not possible," said Agnes in her gentlest tone, "that you yourself may be doing wrong in not going to the home he is providing for you?"

"No, Miss, I don't think it is. The home can wait, and so can George. If he is satisfied, and I am satisfied, what's the use of talking about it?"

"Rachel, my dear, your George is a man of right feeling and good judgment. I will tell you what I should say if I were in his place. 'Here is my dear sweetheart'—I am speaking for him, you know—'Here is my dear sweetheart loving me, and ready to come to me, and here I am ready to commence a new and happy life with the dearest girl in the world. But somebody is keeping us from each other, somebody is separating us. That somebody is a selfish lady, who is doing all she can to prevent my Rachel and me from being happy together. She ought to be ashamed of herself to impose upon a foolish simple girl so.' And George is right, my dear; I am ashamed of myself for acting so. Do you see it as I do?"

"No, Miss," said Rachel, steadily, and somewhat slowly, "if I did I should despise myself; if I did I should not be worthy of any man. O, my dear young lady, you are doing a great wrong by calling yourself selfish, and by thinking what you say. But you don't, you don't! It is only because you don't think of yourself, but only of me, that you are trying to persuade me to leave you. And it is true, is it, that you are doing all you can to keep us apart? Are you not doing everything possible to bring us together a month or two sooner than we want to be? George knows this as well as myself, and if I was to go to him this very day and say, 'Here I am, George; I have left her, and now you can put up the banns,' I believe he'd turn his back upon me, and curl up his lip, and say, 'I don't want you; you're not the girl I took you for.' That's what you'd be doing, Miss; separating us instead of

bringing us together. If you want to do
that——"

And here Rachel broke out into tears, and
her, agitation was more powerful than her
arguments. The two mingled their tears
together, and so for a time there was a break
in this fond battle. But it was only a break.
Agnes renewed it again and again, until at
length George Millington himself spoke to her
about it, and declared that Rachel was acting
with his full and free consent. It must be
confessed that the young fellow was somewhat rueful, for the longing to commence
the new and happy life was strong upon him,
but he spoke up manfully, and whatever
opinion Agnes may have entertained of his
absolute sincerity she was compelled to give
way. Rachel loved him all the more for his
self-denial, and she made it up to him in the
tender courtship between them, looking forward always to the bright future in a way (as
she told him) she never could have thought
of if things had been different.

And now, perhaps it may be supposed that,

after the usual fashion of novelists, the story
will branch out into a dismal record of the
struggles and privations endured by these two
brave and obstinate young women.   But,
happily, there is no need for this, and the writer
is not called upon to invent melancholy inci-
dents and episodes to excite the reader's com-
passion.   Struggles they had, but not greater
than they could cope with.   They had to
work for their living as a matter of course.
The question was, what kind of work they
were fitted for and could obtain, to pay the
necessary expenses of board and lodging.
They succeeded in getting needlework, but
after a month's trial found that it was not
only slavery which would make their young
lives a burden, but that even then they could
not earn sufficient to pay their way.   This
applies especially to Agnes, who could do
dainty, but not rough work, and such delicate
labour with the needle as she was fitted for
was not to be obtained.   It was different
with Rachel.   Putting down figures and
making calculations—you have no idea how

business-like they were in their practical consideration of their position—it was found that Rachel with her needle could earn an average of eight shillings a week, and find time as well to do the cooking and housekeeping. Further than this she had no need, for the earning of these weekly shillings, to work after seven o'clock p.m., and this left her evenings free for George—though she would not have him come every day: she limited him to twice a week, which, after a time, was extended to three evenings out of the seven. Then, about Agnes. Assisted by Mr. Palmer's limited influence, she actually succeeded in securing a footing in a postal telegraph office, where she proved so valuable an acquisition, that she brought home with her every week no less a sum than eighteen shillings. This, with Rachel's eight, made up a total of twenty-six shillings, and upon this they lived as happily as they could expect under the circumstances into which they had been plunged.

It has been indicated and plainly stated

that these two young women were of an obstinate nature. Obstinate may not be the proper term; say, rather, that they were firm in their resolves, and that, having made up their minds as to what it was right to do, they carried out their resolutions with surprising firmness. In this spirit they were equals, and neither could fairly claim the advantage over the other. Instances of Rachel's firmness and remarkable consistency have already been given. We will say a word now of Agnes' conduct in this respect.

Frederick Palmer came home from New Zealand, all his castles in the air tumbled down and extinguished. He went out to make his fortune; he came home penniless, and in feeble health. But the medicine of love, no less than his own manliness and courage, soon restored him, and he put his shoulder to the wheel with a will. Tender and sweet was the first meeting of the lovers, and as tender and sweet was the after communion of two young souls welded together by pure and true affection.

"I have Agnes to work for now," said Frederick to his father. "Money separated us; the want of money unites us. Let us be thankful for poverty."

This was quixotic, but there was a measure of sincerity and absolute thankfulness in it. And shortly after his return to England an astonishing thing occurred. The world, that had been blind so long, suddenly opened its eyes to the undoubted genius of father and son. They painted pictures which were talked of, and the consequence was that they found themselves ascending the ladder. Their paintings were welcomed in the Academy and the galleries, and they had the satisfaction of seeing them hung. Unfortunately they fell into the hands of picture dealers, not in the first rank, and were beguiled by this crew into mortgaging their brushes three years ahead. Only those who have worked for years, hoping against hope, till hope is almost dead, know how easy it is to fall a victim to these sharp dealers. But the Palmers, father and son, were satisfied. The long struggle was over, and fame was theirs, and fortune would be; and for the present their purses were sufficiently filled for their needs.

But love is impatient, and Frederick pleaded for marriage. Agnes listened, and her heart went out to him, but the promise to her father held her back.

" He is not in England," said Frederick, " and you do not know in what part of the world he is to be found. How, then, can you obtain his consent ? "

" It was a solemn promise," Agnes answered, " solemnly given, and I feel that it is binding upon me. It is my duty to wait."

He pleaded, but pleaded in vain ; she was not to be moved. Thus did she rival her faithful maid, Rachel Diprose. All that he could prevail upon her to undertake was that if she could not obtain her father's consent to their union before she was three and twenty, she would ask him to wait no longer. With this he was fain to be content, and Rachel, being informed of her mistress's resolve, communicated it to George Millington, who also

possessed his soul in patience. If he and
Frederick Palmer had compared notes, they
would have agreed that their prospective
brides had remarkable strength of character
and an equally remarkable sense of duty.
Setting marriage aside awhile, they had much
to be thankful for. The course of true love
was running smooth, and a bright future lay
before them.

CHAPTER XXXIX.

HONORIA'S LUCK.

Honoria became a very busy woman indeed after Goodwood; the administration of her affairs occupied her day and night. Before Goodwood she had had enough to do, but she conducted her transactions more privately. Apart from these transactions, some clue to the nature of which will in due time be given, she became more than ever a public character. The extraordinary bets she had made with Louis Redwood leaked out, and were recorded and commented upon in the society papers. She was spoken of as "the lady of Chudleigh," and the strait-laced portion of society were much scandalized by the news that a woman of more than doubtful reputation had come into possession of an estate boasting of an ancient and honourable record. Of the attacks made upon her she took no notice

whatever. That she read them was evident,
for the papers containing them were always
to be found in her house. Probably she was
aware that she had more friends than enemies,
and it is a fact that in many quarters, and
with thousands and thousands of people who
had never beheld her, she was spoken of in
terms of genuine admiration. She was as
deserving of this admiration as of the fainter
censure which pursued her. That her nature
was kind and sympathetic and that an appeal
to her charity was seldom made in vain were
facts which had long been established, but
after the Derby she came out in a new character. No public appeal for money for
charitable purposes was made without her
responding to it, and her name was to be
found in every advertised list of subscriptions.
A number of miners perished in a colliery
explosion, and an appeal for a widows' and
orphans' fund was made, under the auspices
of the Lord Mayor. "Honoria, £50." The
poor-box of a magistrate's court was stated to
be empty. "Honoria, £20." The circum-

stances of a destitute family were brought to light by the harsh and unnecessary summons of a Board School inspector, and some small subscriptions were sent to the magistrate to lift them from poverty. Among these subscriptions, " Honoria, £5." A child's paper asked for help towards a sick cot in a hospital. " Honoria, £10." Other hospitals appealed for funds, and Honoria contributed to all. She made no distinction of race or class, but gave liberally to every one. Like the constant dripping of water, this merciful iteration of her name had its effect in softening the feelings of those who were inclined to judge her harshly; in a certain sense it cut the ground from under their feet, and had an open comparison of their charity and hers been made it would not have resulted favourably to them. The curiosity of strangers grew apace, and the name of Honoria was in everyone's mouth. An article in a society paper went the round of the press in a more or less abridged form. In this article, which was headed, " Honoria and her Charities," a list was given of the amounts she had contributed to benevolent purposes in the course of six weeks; it totted up to £2,000. "This," said the writer, "is at the rate of £18,000 per annum. And we have it on undoubted authority that her private benefactions are on as large-hearted a scale. Who, after this, will venture to whisper a word against her? She sets a noble example to ladies who pride themselves upon their virtue." In these days of publicity such interesting items as this reach all classes of society, from the highest to the lowest, and in the poorer quarters of the city, especially, Honoria was idealized far beyond her deserts or the deserts of any woman. Thus the measure of her popularity could not but be agreeable to her.

In other ways, also, she continued to excite wonder and admiration. After Epsom came Ascot, and there she won more money, some of it from Redwood, who was beginning to be spoken of with bated breath. The knowing ones said, "It is impossible for him to last long at the pace he is going." After Ascot came

Sandown, and her luck continued. Then Kempton, and Sandown again (she did not go to Newmarket), and finally Goodwood; and at all these meetings she added to her store. As she rose, Louis Redwood fell, but he bore his losses with outward equanimity and composure, and paid up without a murmur. It was true that to do this he was compelled to have sudden and secret conferences with his legal agents, Lamb and Freshwater, at which they invariably looked very grave, and shook their heads after his departure; but their alarm at this drifting of his boat of good fortune did not appear to have any effect upon Redwood, who was as haughty and imperious as ever, and would not listen to expostulations. Clerks were kept up all night preparing deeds, which were brought to him early in the morning for his signature; and the spendthrift would afterwards be seen in his usual haunts with unruffled feathers and spirits. It was a peculiar feature in his conduct during these disastrous weeks that, adoring Honoria as he professed, he set himself determinedly against her in all matters of chance or skill upon which money was staked. It was only necessary for her to say that she was going to back a horse at such and such a meeting, and he would immediately offer to lay against it. She took the odds from him, saying lightly, " You may as well lose your money to me as to anyone else." " Better," he replied ; " but I shall beat you yet, my lady." In her house baccarat and roulette were occasionally played ; when she backed red, he backed black, and so with other chances. And her good luck stuck to her and his bad luck stuck to him. They did not play for small stakes ; large sums of money were lost and won. At Goodwood came some " swashing blows." He had a horse in the Steward's Cup ; he backed it and lost. A two-year-old in the Prince of Wales' Stakes cost him a lot of money. He laughed at these reverses, for was he not going to pull it all back, and more, on the Goodwood Cup, in which his horse was favourite at long odds on. The ring, always ready to strip the skin off a man's back, obliged him by taking the odds from him. Honoria, also challenged, accepted what he offered; and the result was that his horse was beaten by a good two lengths. Honoria looked at him curiously at this last stroke, and for the first time she saw his lips twitch. But he recovered himself almost immediately, and, with a dare-devil laugh, asked her if she was coming to the paddock. On the way, he said;

"Did it ever occur to you that I might one day commit murder?"

"Not exactly that," she replied. "Your courage would fail you at the last moment."

When she saw him look at the renowned jockey Beane, who rode his horses and could win for other owners and not for him, she knew what he meant. She herself had a suspicion that Beane was "selling" his master in the interests of certain bookmakers, and had often wondered why Redwood did not put up some other jockey. She had, indeed, expressed this wonder to him, not imagining that her doubt of the jockey's honesty was

sufficient to make Redwood stick to him all
the closer.

Meanwhile all Chudleigh was in a state of
the greatest excitement. The village was
once more alive. Relays of workmen made
their appearance, and the old house and the
park were put in thorough order. Money was
spent freely, and the inhabitants, who had
fallen into the dullest of trances, suddenly
shook themselves awake and behaved with
animation. The landlord of " The Brindled
Cow " polished up his pots and glasses, and
briskly bestirred himself. For were not his
bar and taproom thronged with the men
Honoria's agents had sent down to put the
place in order for her, and was not his till
resounding with the chink of silver and
copper? " It is like old times come again,"
he said, rubbing his hands. " And as sure as
I'm alive there's my old friend, Simpson!"
There was his old friend Simpson truly, holding out his hand to him and asking how he
was. Simpson had been lent by Louis Redwood to Honoria, and was in Chudleigh now

upon her business and in her interests. There was no newspaper in the sleepy village, and the world's affairs were so far apart from the inhabitants of Chudleigh that they did not trouble themselves about them. They had heard nothing of Honoria coming into possession of the estate; all that they knew was that the Haldanes had lost it, and that the Hall had been empty ever since.

The landlord of "The Brindled Cow" did not find Simpson over communicative; Simpson had been warned not to let his tongue run too freely, and to be especially reticent as to who the new owner of the estate really was. He would have been better pleased if no restriction had been put upon him, but he knew how to extract some tribute in the way of self-importance from the mystery.

"You're the very man we want," said the landlord, after inviting Simpson to a drink. "What sort of a family is it that's coming to the Hall? Is it a large family? Are they going to keep here? Are they rich? Are they free with their money?"

" Can't answer all your questions," said Simpson, " my position being a confidential one, you know. But you shall see what you shall see. Don't let it go any further, but it's a lady that's now the master. That's between you and me. As for being free with her money, the Haldanes weren't in it with her."

" That's enough for me," said the landlord blithely.

" There's to be a house-warming," said Simpson ; " lot's of company ; any number of swells."

" That sounds promising. A man might as well be dead as alive in the times we've gone through lately. When are they coming ? "

" About the end of August," said Simpson. " Exact date not fixed yet."

And then, after partaking of another drink at the landlord's expense, Simpson went to the Hall to see how things were getting along there.

CHAPTER XL.

It was during the second week in August that Honoria met with an adventure. She was shopping in Regent Street, and, her purchases made, was about to step into her carriage when the figures of two persons attracted her attention. One was our friend Mr. Millington, the other an elderly woman in rags whom she did not know. Both were gazing at her, but in different ways. Pity, curiosity, and a certain quality of admiration were expressed in Mr. Millington's eyes, and a hungering greediness in the eyes of the woman. This latter might have been caused by the contrast between them, Honoria representing wealth and luxury, the elderly woman representing the uttermost depth of poverty. Honoria gave her a shilling, and, pausing a moment, beckoned to Mr. Millington, who, till then, had made no movement towards her.

" It is a long time since we met," she said, holding out her hand to him. " Would you mind stepping into my carriage with me? "

" I had rather not," said Mr. Millington. " If you wish to speak to me you can do so here."

It was a rebuke, and Honoria accepted it as such, but she made no comment upon it.

" It will not hurt you," she said, " to walk a little way with me."

" No," he replied, " I will do that."

They crossed the road, and Honoria led the way to a quieter street. The raggedly-dressed woman followed them at a little distance.

" Mr. Millington," said Honoria, " you see I do not forget your name—I am in your debt."

" I am not aware of it."

" You must remember the night you took me from Chudleigh to London ? "

" I remember it very well."

" You paid for my fare, and spent money

42*

upon me.   I owe you that much at all events."

" The money was repaid to me."

" By a lady ? "

" By a lady."

" It cannot do her any harm if I mention her name.   Miss Haldane ? "

" Yes.   Miss Haldane."

" Heaven reward her !   I showed her great ingratitude.   I do not seek to excuse myself, Mr. Millington, and though I do not deserve your respect, it would be charitable to pity me."

" I do sincerely pity you."

" Thank you.   Have you seen Miss Haldane lately ? "

" I see her frequently."

" Is she in London, then ? "

" She has been in London for some time."

" I trust she is happy."

" She is as happy as she can be in her circumstances."

" You cannot mean that she is poor ? "

" If you have any other subject to speak

of," said Mr. Millington, " do so, please. I
cannot continue this."

" You are right," said Honoria with a sigh.
" Mr. Millington, I think no one in London
knows me as I know myself. Even when
you say you pity me, you do it only out of
compliment, and to save yourself from saying
something harder."

" You are wrong : I do honestly pity you."

" I see Mr. Haldane every day," said
Honoria, " and he does not mention his
daughter's name. I hear he is not friendly
with her. It is this, perhaps, that renders
her less happy than she should be. In an
indirect manner, Mr. Millington, I have shown
some recognition of her kindness towards me.
It has been my good fortune to be in a position to extend a helping hand to some poor
persons, and to distribute a small portion of
what has fallen to my share among those who
are struggling with misfortune. It is the
memory of her goodness that has urged me to
this and that will urge me to do it as long as
it is in my power. It could not come out of

my own nature, because I am thoroughly bad. Perhaps you will remember what I say when all the world turns its back upon me—as it did once before in my life—all the world but her. Mr. Millington, I have been thinking lately of writing to you and asking you to do me a service."

" I cannot see in what way I can be of service to you," said Mr. Millington, stiffly.

" It may be also rendering a service to two poor women in trouble, though that is not my only motive. I will not go into any further explanation, because you would neither understand nor sympathize with me. I thought it likely that you might recommend me to a reliable person who could obtain some information for me."

" Some information respecting others?"

" Yes."

" You want an inquiry agent?"

" Yes, an honest man."

" There are plenty of them. Why come to me?"

" Because I want a man upon whom I can

thoroughly rely.   It is a matter so delicate that I would rather not go to an entire stranger.   Will you oblige me ? "

"I must first know the name of the women you refer to," said Mr. Millington.   He was not disposed to trust Honoria, and he had a suspicion that she had Miss Haldane and Rachel Diprose in her mind.

"I will tell you willingly.   Their name is Kennedy, and they live in Wellington Street, South Lambeth."

"Mrs. Kennedy and her daughter!" exclaimed Mr. Millington.

"You are acquainted with them?"

"No, but a friend of mine is, and strangely enough he is an inquiry agent, and in former years did some business for Mrs. Kennedy in connection with Mr. Haldane."

The name escaped his lips before he could check its utterance.   It was Honoria's turn now to be surprised.

"That is very singular," she said, "and it makes me all the more anxious.   He may be the very man I want.   I beg that you will not refuse me. I assure you my motive is a good one."

"I will be frank with you," said Mr. Millington. "On the night before the Derby my friend and I were in the Royal Palace of Pleasure, and witnessed the accident to the lad whom you befriended and took to South Lambeth in your carriage. My friend heard you give the address—it was 7, Wellington Street, I think —and we followed you there. After you entered the house we saw Mrs. Kennedy come from it, with some work she was taking home." He paused a moment or two before he spoke again. "I will give you his address. His name is Barlow. He took the greatest interest in Mrs. Kennedy's commission, which was only relinquished because she had no money to prosecute it. It is likely he will be glad to take it up again. If he does, and carries it, with your help, to a successful issue, you will be the means of doing justice to one who has been grievously wronged." He wrote Mr. Barlow's name and address on a card, and gave it to Honoria.

"Is he in his office now, Mr. Millington?" she asked.

"I think you will find him there."

"Do you live in the same house to which you took me on the night you brought me from Chudleigh?"

" Yes."

"Thank you.   Perhaps you will not mind taking my card.   You may wish to say something to me on this or some other matter. Mr. Millington, you have laid me under another deep obligation to you.   I am rich ; money is no object to me.   Should you desire to serve any one and will come to me I shall be more than ever indebted to you."

He stood with her card in his hand looking after her as she walked towards Regent Street. So interested and engrossed was he in following her movements that the card slipped from his hand.   The raggedly-dressed woman who had not removed her eyes from them during the interview, darted forward and picked it up.

"Yes," she mumbled, reading the name and

address, "Honoria.   It is Honoria!"   A
doubt crossed her mind.   "But there may be
more than one of that name."

"The card, please," said Mr. Millington,
but she put her hand behind her back.

"She is a grand lady—a grand lady!   You
know her, kind sir?"

"I know something of her.   I will trouble
you for the card."

"Don't be in such a hurry, kind sir.   She
wouldn't thank you for it.   What do you
know of her?   Where she comes from, eh?
Tell me that, kind sir."

"Indeed I shall not tell you.   It can be no
concern of yours."

"If you won't tell me," cried the woman,
"I'll tell you.   What do you say to Chudleigh, kind sir?"

"Come, come," said Mr. Millington, "you
are not the only one who knows that.   The
lady gave you a shilling; here's another for
you.   Now hand me that card.   I want the
address."

"So do I, so do I—and my memory's not so

good as it was.   Would you mind writing it
down for me?"

Had he not wished to avoid a scene and
get away, Mr. Millington would have refused,
so for his own sake, more than that of the
wretched woman before him, he wrote the
address on the back of an envelope, and
recovered the card.

" Would you like me to tell you, kind sir,"
said the woman, " where she came from before
she went to Chudleigh?   What do you say to
Bittern?"

Mr. Millington's memory was not in the
same condition as hers, and he recollected
that Bittern was the village mentioned by
Simpson on his first introduction to Honoria
in Chudleigh, as being the place she lived in
when quite a little child, with a woman who
suddenly disappeared and left her to the
mercy of the world.   Was this the woman?
This mental question caused him to tarry
awhile.

" Are you a native of Bittern?" he asked.

" No, kind sir."

"Of Chudleigh?"

"No, kind sir. I am London born and London bred."

"But you lived in Bittern a good many years ago, taking care of a child?"

She gave a Roland for his Oliver. "That is no concern of yours," she said. "I've got a secret to sell. It might be worth money, now she's a fine lady. Who knows—who knows?"

She was hurrying away when he stopped her. "A moment, my good woman. You are not overburdened with money."

"I'm very poor, very poor, kind sir," she whined.

"I will give you," said Mr. Millington, producing his purse, "a shilling each if you will answer two questions, two simple, innocent questions."

It was a tempting offer; these shillings represented fine gold in the eyes of the poverty-stricken woman; and yet she paused.

"Depends upon what they are, kind sir."

"You did live in Bittern some years ago, and a little child was in your care?"

"That's the two questions," she said, with cunning.

"I mean it as one. The second will follow."

"Yes, kind sir, I did. Give me a shilling."

"Not till you have answered the second question. Was that child — a girl — your own?"

"Was I her mother? No, kind sir. Give me two shillings."

He gave her the money, and she went away. He looked after her thoughtfully, as he had looked after Honoria. It was only when she was out of sight that he recollected that Mr. Haldane was the man who, under a false name, had betrayed the woman who was now passing as Mrs. Kennedy's daughter. Much disturbed in his mind, he walked slowly home.

CHAPTER XLI.

THE LADY OF CHUDLEIGH.

On the 25th of August, Honoria made her entrance into Chudleigh. On the day previous Louis Redwood was closeted with his legal advisers—Messrs. Lamb and Freshwater.

" We are bound to lay these matters before you, sir," said Mr. Lamb, who was the spokesman of the firm.

"I suppose there's no help for it," said Louis Redwood, " but it is an infernal nuisance for all that."

" It is not quite the way to look at it," responded Mr. Lamb.

" It is the way I look at it," retorted Redwood.

Mr. Lamb was a lawyer of the old school, and a gentleman of the old school. He still wore the frilled shirt and the high stock, and though his clothes were made by a modern

tailor, they were of the old cut and style. He
would wear no other, and it added to the
respect in which he was borne by clients as
old, but not as old-fashioned, as himself.

"The vital question now is," said Mr. Lamb,
"what is to be done?"

Mr. Freshwater nodded, and his lips moved.
He was mutely repeating his partner's words,
"What is to be done?"

"That," replied Redwood, "is a question
for you to answer."

"It is a question, sir," said Mr. Lamb,
"that we have been asking for several years."

"And a question," said Mr. Redwood,
"that you have always answered, and
answered satisfactorily."

"Everything," observed Mr. Lamb, "comes
to an end."

"Comes to an end," mutely repeated Mr.
Freshwater. It was the part he played in
interviews of this nature.

"A fine estate," continued Mr. Lamb, as
Louis Redwood leant back in his chair,
chewing a cigar, "wasted, squandered, I may

say. A noble fortune which should now be standing at double the amount it was instead of standing at zero."

"Zero," said Louis Redwood, "has been the ruin of many good fellows."

"Will you look over these papers, sir?"

"Psha! What would be the use? I am perfectly satisfied with your figures. I have never questioned them. If I devote a week to an examination of them, it would not alter the result."

"It would not, sir. They are here, however, for your examination, at any time, or for the examination of any person you may appoint. Have you at the present moment any idea of the extent of your fortune on the day you came of age?"

"At the present moment I have no idea whatever. At the present moment I have only one wish, that the fortune was as great to-day as it was on the day I came of age."

"We echo that wish, sir, with all our hearts."

" Mr. Freshwater mutely repeated, " With all our hearts."

" But that," said Redwood, " is an idle wish. Picking up spilt milk. Quite out of the question."

" Entirely. Your income, in round numbers, sir, when you came of age, was eighty-two thousand pounds. Where has it all gone to ? "

" Echo answers," said Redwood.

" It was not our duty to dictate. Simply to advise. Occasionally to remonstrate."

" Time thrown away, I am afraid."

" Entirely thrown away, as to our sorrow we learned. You are aware, sir," said Mr. Lamb, waving his hand with a slow pathetic motion over the table which was strewn with papers, " what these spell now."

" Tell me."

" They spell ruin."

" They spell ruin," mutely repeated Mr. Freshwater.

" Absolute ? "

" Absolute."

" To the last thousand ? "

" Perhaps not quite that. There is your estate in Warwickshire, upon which there is only a first mortgage. The property is increasing in value."

Louis Redwood laughed. " I knew there was something left—always a chestnut in the fire."

" The last, sir, the last."

" I have heard that before. Your friendly interest in my welfare makes you take too melancholy a view. There is something still more beside the Warwickshire estate. Come, confess now, Mr. Lamb."

" What I have done in earlier days affords no criterion. I assure you there is nothing else left."

" On your honour as a gentleman ? "

" On my honour as a gentleman."

" That settles it. A second mortgage, now, on the Warwickshire estate. How much can you raise ? "

" I beg you to consider, sir."

" I decline. Money I must have. It is

increasing in value, you say. Borrow to the hilt. You have made inquiries, I know, and some sharp fellow is ready to plank the money down. How much?"

"Fifteen thousand," said Mr. Lamb, with a sigh.

"I can break the bank a dozen times over with that amount. But I've a better diggings than Monte Carlo. Doncaster, Mr. Lamb, Doncaster. Do you know what will win the Leger? I do, and I'll put a monkey on for you; but I'm forgetting—you never bet. Not my own horse this time, Mr. Lamb. I can get ten to one, ten to one. Before a month has gone by that fifteen thousand will be a hundred thousand, and when once the ball is set rolling it goes on rolling. It's a mathematical certainty that the luck must turn if you don't desert your colours. Mr. Lamb, borrow that money for me immediately, without a day's delay, and pay it in to my credit. I am going to Chudleigh to-morrow, and shall be at the Manor Hall till the eighth of next month. I will run up to London to

43*

sign the deeds, or you can send them down
to me. Whichever you please. Meanwhile
you can oblige me by paying in to my bank a
couple of thousand—say three. Is that understood?"

"We can do what you wish, sir; but this
will be the end."

"Will be the end," repeated Mr. Freshwater.

"Not by a long way," said Redwood,
shaking hands with his advisers. "Never
prophesy until you know."

Honoria's entrance into Chudleigh was an
event destined to live in the memory of the
oldest inhabitant, whoever that may be.
With the exception of those who lived at the
Rectory every man and woman turned out to
welcome her. The small windows of the
cottages that lined the narrow road leading to
the park were bright with flowers, and everything was sweet and fresh and trim. It had
been her intention at first to go down by
train, but she had been persuaded into adopt-
ing the more public entry upon her property,

for it was really hers now, and she was the
landlady of half the humble cottages she
passed.

"It will look like sneaking into the Hall,"
Redwood said, "and as if you were ashamed
of being seen there."

That remark decided her. How well she
remembered every nook and corner in the
village, and the last night she had spent
there! She was very quiet as she rode along;
there was no pride in her face. Its expression
was sad even to sternness, and Louis Redwood
remarked it with surprise.

"What has come over you?" he asked.
"You are a changed woman."

"Yes, I am changed," she replied, and her
voice was hard and cold. "I have made a
strange discovery this last week. I have
never till now realized how thoroughly base
and wicked a man can be."

He chimed in with her humour. "We are
a bad lot," he said, "but we are what we are
made to be, I suppose."

"What we are made to be!" she said

musingly. "Yes, what we are made to be.
Redwood, if a man did' you a mortal injury,
if he ruined your life and brought you down
to the gutter, if through his act people looked
upon him with contempt and scorn instead of
respect, if by his cowardice and treachery he
poisoned your blood and made a shame and
a by-word of you, would you forgive him ? "

Redwood's face darkened. "Are you
thinking of me," he asked, "and do you
want me to trap myself? "

"I am not thinking of you, but of another
man."

"Then drive him down, and pay the debt
you owe him !" he cried savagely.

"I must find some way to do this. Can I
count upon your assistance ? "

"There is nothing you bid me do that I will
shrink from."

It was he/who was the beggar now, it was
he who implored and entreated, and whose
fate seemed to hang upon her words, as her
fate had once hung upon his. They had
changed places. She ruled, and he was at

her feet, at the feet of the outcast he had spurned and taunted in Chudleigh Woods.

"You have your revenge," he said, as the women of the village curtseyed and locks were pulled in servile obeisance.

"I take no pleasure in it," she said. "I would like to know what is in their hearts."

"I would like to know what is in yours."

"You may soon."

He caught at her words, twisting hope out of them.

"Do you mean it, Honoria?"

"I have never in my life been more in earnest, and that must content you. Don't pester me with questions; I must work my mood out my own way, which," she added, with a touch of her old self, "is a wilful way, as you have found out long since."

"You are a witch," he said, "and I was a fool, once upon a time. But it's never too late to learn, I hope."

"I have a little surprise in store," she said, presently, "for some who will be my

guests this week at the Hall, and I shall have
a little secret which I must keep to myself till
the time comes to reveal it. You have
promised your assistance. If you fail, or cross
me, I will never speak another word to you.
Remember that."

He repeated his assurance of obedience,
and then they talked of other matters.

The following day the guests began to
arrive, and Honoria welcomed them as though
she had been born into the state in which she
so strangely found herself. There was no
awkwardness in her manners, and she and
those she had invited were quite at home
with each other. Mr. Haldane was there,
and feeling himself called upon to play a
part as strange as that of Honoria, he
succeeded in concealing his feelings. His
worldly condition had not improved. His
passion for gambling kept him poor, and on
three separate occasions Honoria had lent
him money. He was in need of a loan now,
but Honoria held off somewhat, and told him
he must wait.

"You shall have more than you ask for,"
she said, "before our party breaks up."

He smiled his thanks, and she suddenly
turned her face from him to conceal the expression of loathing which flashed into it at
his fawning. But though he did not see it he
thought her manner strange, and he spoke of
it to Redwood.

"She is in a queer temper," said Redwood:
"she told me so herself. Leave her alone;
she'll soon come round."

The guests were all men: there was not a
female among them; men of the world, men
about town, drawn together by a certain
magnetism, and behaving decorously and with
propriety, and yet with a freedom which
would not have obtained in the restraining
presence of ladies.

On the first night of this gathering an
incident occurred of which only one of the
guests was cognizant. All the men, with the
exception of Major Causton, were playing
cards or billiards. The hour was eleven, and
the excitement of the gambling kept the men

together.   Outside on the lawn Honoria and
Major Causton were holding watch.

"You will not betray me?" said Honoria.

"As a man of honour and a gentleman,"
said Major Causton, his hand on his heart,
"your secret is mine, and shall not pass my
lips."

Her own lips curled when he made this
reference to himself as a gentleman and a
man of honour, but she was satisfied with his
assurance.   She was to pay him well for such
services as she needed from him.   If he
betrayed her his purse would be so much the
lighter.   To an impecunious man this fact
was a sufficiently strong chain.

"Hark!" said Honoria.   "I think I hear
them."

It was the sound of wheels she heard.   The
sound came closer, and at a signal from
Causton, who had gone forward, a carriage
with the windows down stopped within fifty
yards of the house.   Two women, one support-
ing the other, alighted from the carriage, and
Honoria stepped lightly up to them, and

passed her arm round the weaker of the two. The hall door was open.

" See if all is safe," said Honoria to Major Causton, " and wave your handkerchief if no one is about."

The handkerchief was waved, and Honoria and her companions passed into the house, and ascended the stairs to the left wing, the apartments in which were devoted solely to Honoria's use. On the top of the staircase Honoria turned towards Major Causton, who was standing at the foot. She put her finger to her lips. Causton nodded, and the three women went into their apartments.

CHAPTER XLII.

On the following day none of the guests saw their hostess. Neither at breakfast nor at dinner did she make her appearance, and the men looked at each other and asked Mr. Haldane and Louis Redwood the reason of her absence. These gentlemen, however, could give no satisfactory reply to the inquiry, being as much in the dark as their companions. Privately they questioned Simpson, who knew little, but suspected much. Accustomed to pry slyly into matters which did not immediately concern himself he had ascertained that there had been sent into Honoria's apartments more than sufficient food for one person. Honoria had brought with her to the Hall a female servant entirely devoted to her, and upon whose secrecy she could rely.

This woman waited upon her mistress, and not one of the other servants was allowed to enter the rooms which Honoria had set apart for her own use. She took the trays and dishes from the attendants who brought them from the kitchen, and waited until they had descended the stairs before she carried the food into her mistress' apartments, and in all her movements the same air of secrecy was observed. Simpson made an endeavour to ingratiate himself into her confidence, but she would exchange no words with him. "Very mysterious," said he to himself, and, his curiosity whetted, he applied himself to the task of elucidating the mystery. He was so far successful as to become convinced that there were other occupants in the left wing besides Honoria and her servant, but his discoveries did not extend beyond this. Such as they were he communicated them to his master Louis Redwood, who could make nothing of them.

"She is beyond me, Haldane," he said "Perhaps she has a surprise in store for us."

Mr. Haldane had cogent reasons for wishing to see Honoria. The gambling on the previous night had been heavy, and he had lost a large sum of money, for which he had given his paper, payable on demand. He had no means to meet his obligations, and he depended upon Honoria's half-promise to put him in funds. He sent a note to her, and received no reply. However, his creditors did not press him, and on the second night he played with them again, and again lost heavily. During the daytime the guests did pretty much as they liked; smoked, rode, played billiards, and made excursions into the woods and grounds. It was not until night that serious play was indulged in. Honoria had privately put every one of them on good behaviour, otherwise the villagers would very likely have been scandalized.

At noon on the third day the guests, talking among themselves, discussed Honoria's absence, and decided that it was altogether too bad for her to keep herself aloof from

them.   Redwood mentioned Simpson's suspi-
cions, that she had friends in her apartments
to whom they had not been introduced.
Simpson was called, and questioned.   He had
seen nothing, but he had heard voices.
" Men's voices?" they asked.   " No," replied
Simpson, " women's."   They agreed that the
affair was growing very strange, and one
among them suggested that they should send
a " round robin " to Honoria, in the shape of
a petition, begging her to favour them with
her presence, and to favour them, also, with
an introduction to the ladies for whom she
had deserted them.   To this petition, which
was signed by all her guests, Honoria returned
a reply that she would meet them in the
music-room (an apartment specially fitted for
large receptions) in the course of a quarter of
an hour.   They thronged round her on her
entrance, but she waved them away with a
gesture of command which was instantly
obeyed.   One end of the music-room was
slightly raised, so that, standing there, Honoria,
who was above the ordinary stature of women,

topped the tallest of her guests by an inch or two. They noted a change in her. During the last few days she seemed to have grown years older; there was a stern expression upon her face, and her eyes, travelling around, dwelt a moment with aversion upon the figure of Mr. Haldane, who had taken up his position to the left of her. She commenced to speak abruptly.

" It is scarcely courteous of me," she said, " that I should invite you here, and then, as you say, desert you. I hope there has been nothing wanting."

They answered in various ways that everything was perfection, that her hospitality was princely, that if the Hall were their own they could not expect better treatment, and that the only thing they had to complain of was that she should absent herself from them.

" I had a motive," she said, " which I do not intend to keep from you much longer. You are right in your surmise that I have lady friends in my private apartments to whom

you have not been introduced. Only one of
the gentlemen present is acquainted with
these ladies, and it is scarcely fair that he
should possess a privilege from which the
others are debarred. I propose to make you
all acquainted with them this evening after
dinner. I take it that you are all men of
honour."

They became grave instantly, and nodded.
Even the shadiest amongst them did not hesitate to claim the title.

"It is a delicate matter," said Honoria,
"and I believe I shall surprise and interest
you in certain disclosures I propose to make
to you after dinner. I wish to enlist your
sympathies, your manliness, all that is best
within you, in the cause of suffering and
unmerited misfortune. Who will be my
knights?"

They cried with one voice that all would.
They had not the smallest understanding of
her meaning, but they imagined that she had
some amusing novelty with which she intended to entertain them.

" I wish you," she pursued, " to elect six gentlemen as a Council of Honour, who shall in some sense occupy the position of judges in what I have to disclose."

" Are we not to hear it ? " they asked.

" Yes," she replied, " all of you. Indeed, I shall exact a promise that you are all present, and that not one of you shall leave the room till I have finished what I have to say."

" Jove ! " cried a guest. " It is like a romance."

" A sad romance," said Honoria. " Say, rather, a page out of life's history. Do you all promise to let me do what I wish in my own way, and not to thwart me ? I ask it as a favour."

The eldest gentleman there said it was not a favour she asked, it was a right, and that they would pledge themselves unhesitatingly, in testimony of which he called upon them to hold up their hands. Every hand was held up.

" The man who forfeits his word," said

Honoria, "is unworthy the name of gentleman. Now if you please, we will adjourn. We shall meet again at dinner."

"And your lady friends?" they asked.

"You will see them afterwards. We dine at eight. At ten I shall expect to see you all here in this room."

These words were intended as a dismissal, and they filed out. Two lingered behind, Louis Redwood and Mr. Haldane.

"What is all this mystery about, Honoria?" inquired Redwood.

"You will learn to-night. I answer no questions now. Mr. Haldane, I should like a moment or two with you."

"That is an order to me to go," said Redwood savagely. "Well, it will be all one in a hundred years. Haldane, you will find me in the billiard room."

He swung away in a furious temper. Slowly and surely Honoria seemed to be slipping from him.

"You sent me a note," said Honoria to Mr. Haldane, when they were alone, "asking for

44*

money. I did not reply, because you are already sufficiently in my debt."

"But you promised me," said Mr. Haldane, uneasily.

"Not exactly. I think I said that before our party breaks up you should have more than you bargained for. That can hardly be construed into a promise. Mr. Haldane, do you think you have any claim upon me?"

"Only upon your kindness."

"You have no real claim upon me?"

"None that I know of."

"It is I, perhaps, who have a claim upon you. Do not interrupt me. You will hear stranger things than that before we have done with each other. You lost heavily last night?"

"I did, and the night before as well. Ill luck has dogged me all my life."

"It is unfortunate; and you have done nothing to deserve it?"

"Nothing whatever."

Honoria's fixed gaze brought the colour to his cheeks. A scornful laugh escaped her.

He could not meet her gaze, and he looked down nervously.

"It must be painful to you, Mr. Haldane," she said presently, " to find yourself merely a guest where once you were master."

" Do you think I have not suffered enough without reminding me of it ? " he cried, with a movement of despair.

" Others have suffered also; but it is not of this matter I wish to speak just now. You have given your paper for your losses these last two nights."

" Have they been blabbing about it ? " he asked sulkily.

" It has reached my ears. How much have you lost ? "

" Eight hundred pounds."

" And you owe me six. That makes fourteen hundred. It is the price I am willing to pay for something I will purchase of you."

Mr. Haldane caught his breath, and a moment afterwards said bitterly, "I did not know I possessed anything of such value. I should like to hear what it is."

"You have a daughter in London, Miss Agnes Haldane, of whom we spoke a little time ago."

"If she were my property," said Mr. Haldane, in a brutal tone, "I would sell her to you for that sum with pleasure."

"Of that I have very little doubt," said Honoria, steadily. "Anyone acquainted with your history would give you credit for just so much feeling."

"You are safe in insulting me," he remarked.

"Between you and me there can be no question of insult. We have an account to settle, and when it is settled the balance against you will be one you cannot wipe off."

He thought she referred to the money she had already given him, and he was silent, conscious that, apart from this fourteen hundred pounds, he was humiliatingly in her debt. Then it occurred to him that one of the ladies in her private apartments to whom they were to be introduced that night might be his daughter. He put the question to her, and she answered plainly that his daughter Agnes was not in Chudleigh.

"So you will not sell," she added, and turned as if about to leave him.

"You have not told me what it is you wish to buy," he said quickly, stepping before her.

"It is simply your consent to Miss Haldane's marriage with Mr. Frederick Palmer, the gentleman she loves and to whom she is engaged."

"Oh, that!" he exclaimed, with a frown. "You seem to know a great deal about me."

"More than you are aware of," she rejoined. "My time is valuable. Do you sell?"

It was imperative that he should pay the debt he had incurred, and there was no other way. Clear once more, there was still a chance, his credit remaining good, of his winning a big stake from the men with whom he was in association.

"I sell," he said. "I presume you will

yourself convey this precious consent of mine to my daughter."

"I shall have nothing to do with it," she said. "You will write a letter to her, removing the ban you placed upon her happiness. I stipulate that my name shall not be mentioned."

"I will write to her in the course of the day, and I will send the letter when I obtain her address."

"You will write to her now, in this room, before you leave me. I will give you her address."

"You do not trust me; you will not take my word?"

"Good God!" she cried, striking with her hand the chair by which she was standing. "What woman would, knowing what I know?"

He turned white to his lips. Passing his hand across his forehead he raised his eyes to her face, upon which horror and contempt were expressed. The face of the woman he had betrayed and degraded rose to his mind.

Appalled by the memory of his treachery, he whispered,

"Who and what are you?"

"Write the letter," she said, pointing to a table, upon which were writing materials. "What I purchase of you to-day for fourteen hundred pounds will not be worth fourteen pence to-morrow."

He spoke no more, but moving to the table, wrote the following letter, which he handed to her:

"My dear Daughter,—

"You gave me a promise that you would not marry Mr. Frederick Palmer without my consent. I am pleased now to give you my consent to your union with that gentleman.

"Your affectionate father,

"C. HALDANE."

Honoria read the letter, and handing it back to him, dictated the address, which he also wrote.

"Put the letter in the envelope, and fasten it," she said. "I will see that it is delivered. Here is a cheque for eight hundred pounds, and my receipt for the money you owe me."

In silence he took the papers from her hand, and with a last cowardly look at her left the room.

CHAPTER XLIII.

RETRIBUTION.

NOT one of those present in the music room of the Manor Hall on this night was likely ever to forget the scene of which he was a witness. During the hours before dinner there had been a great deal of conversation with respect to what Honoria had said to them in the morning, and they asked one another for an explanation of the mystery. No satisfactory information, however, could be given by any of the guests, although Honoria's statement that there was one among them who was acquainted with the ladies to whom they were to be introduced was frequently quoted. Louis Redwood was questioned, and declared that he knew nothing whatever of them; Mr. Haldane declared the same; but both these gentlemen were stirred by an uneasy feeling that the surprise Honoria had in store for her guests was destined to be in some way unpleasant to themselves. Major Causton, who was known to be in Honoria's confidence, was also closely questioned, but he declared upon his honour that although he knew of the presence of two strange ladies in the house, he had no idea who they were, and had, in fact, not seen their faces. Honoria's desire that six of their body should be elected as a Council of Honour was much discussed ; they laughed at it rather, but felt bound to carry out her wish. The difficult point to decide was whom should they select. Eventually it was decided that the election should be by ballot, and among the six gentlemen so elected were the friends, Louis Redwood and Mr. Haldane. " Bound to vote for you, old fellow," they said to Mr. Haldane, " for you were once master here. Devilish hard luck to lose such an estate."

At the dinner table, where Honoria, as she had promised, made her appearance, she was asked what form the entertainment she had provided for them would take, and her reply was that it would take the form of a story.

"Only a story, Honoria!" protested a gentleman. "I was in hopes that you were going to give us a romance."

"Some persons might even call it that," said Honoria; "but whatever it is you will find it sufficiently interesting."

When, at ten o'clock, all the guests being assembled in the music-room, she made her entrance, a buzz of admiration went round. Her dress, her beauty, her jewels, were the theme of general admiration. "Gad!" cried an elderly roue. "She deserves her position." The names of her Council of Honour were submitted to her, and her eyes gleamed as they rested upon the names of Mr. Haldane and Louis Redwood. She inquired how the selection had been made, and was informed by ballot.

"Do you believe in fate, gentlemen?" she asked. Some did, and some did not. "There is something like fatality," she added,

" in Mr. Haldane and Mr. Redwood being on the Council. They might have to sit in judgment on themselves."

They said that this would make the proceeding all the more interesting, and then Honoria asked them to be seated, and, standing, held up her hand for silence.

" The story I have to tell," she commenced, " is a story of real life. It begins, as most other stories do, I suppose, with one man and one woman.

" The woman, at that time a young girl, with no experience of the world such as we possess, was living in the home of a lady who had adopted her, and who loved her as a daughter. She was foolishly ignorant and foolishly simple. The man was a man of the world, who I have no doubt had already had many adventures and experiences. He was so clever as to be able to overmatch simplicity, and he succeeded here as doubtless he succeeded elsewhere. A year after they first met they were living together, and they were not man and wife."

The gentlemen shifted rather awkwardly on their chairs. Their hostess was telling them, so far, nothing new or novel, but to hear the familiar story told in plain, direct language by a woman, and such a woman as Honoria, was an entirely new experience to them, and stirred up feelings which they would rather had lain dormant.

"Of course," she proceeded, " he had promised her marriage, and of course had not fulfilled his promise. But for a little time she believed herself to be a wife, because he had so far satisfied her scruples as to go through some ceremony with her in a private house which she understood to be legally binding. I have told you that she was a simple, foolish girl, but she is not the only one who has trusted a man's word and has been deceived.

" The ceremony I speak of took place in America, where the man had followed the woman. Mr. Haldane, may I inquire if my story is wearying you ? "

Mr. Haldane, white and trembling, had involuntarily risen to his feet, but at this direct question he became aware that general attention was drawn to him, and with an attempt to regain his self-possession, he jauntily waved his hand, and resumed his seat. He could not, however, sufficiently command his voice to reply. Honoria continued :

" In England it would have been more difficult to carry out such a deception. In America, where the woman was an entire stranger, he found it comparatively easy. I must mention another circumstance in connection with my story ; the man played his part under an assumed name.

" Beginning to be tired of his victim, he returned to England in her company. They lived for a little while in London. From London they went to Paris, and there the woman learned that she was not married, and there a child was born, a girl.

" And there the man deserted the woman, and left her to perish. From that time until the present moment she has never seen the face of the villain who ruined her life.

" I perfectly understand what I am saying. I perfectly understand my position. I know the place I hold in the world, and I am aware that there are shameful points of resemblance between this woman and myself. Pray do not interrupt me, or you will make the task I have set myself, and intend to perform, more difficult than it already is. I am speaking plainly for various reasons, one of which is that our acquaintance ends this night. Thanking you for the trouble I have put you to in visiting this house, I beg that you will to-morrow morning leave me to a duty I see before me.

" I must not do injustice to the man I have spoken of. When he deserted the woman in Paris he did not leave her to die in want. He employed agents, through whom he contributed to her support. He did not think she would live long to trouble him. In this he was mistaken. The woman is now living.

" But there is a moral as well as a physical death. This kind of death came to the woman.

" Weak, foolish, despairing, she took to drink. You know what that means. Am I not speaking plainly?

" There is one law for a man, and another law for a woman. The woman of my story fell. The man retained his place. She crawled through the world; he went, smiling, through it. This is called justice.

" I perceive that Mr. Haldane continues to be restless and disturbed. If he doubts my story, if he thinks it is a jest I am playing upon him, let me inform him that I am a living proof of its truth.

" It has not often happened that a woman, wronged by a man as this woman was, is able to turn the tables upon him. It happens now and here.

" Alone, helpless, degraded, the woman crawled her way through the world. She even lost her child; she was told it died. It was false. The child lived, and lives.

" I promised to introduce you to two
ladies who are living with me here in a state
of seclusion. I am about to redeem my
promise.

" Before I do so let me confess that in
asking you to elect a Council of Honour I
was hardly in earnest. Even if it were not a
sad joke I should decline to accept two of the
persons you have named. You, and they,
will know to whom I refer. The Council,
therefore, does not exist, not being com-
petent, as a body, to decide a question of
honour. If they were, it would not alter the
story I have told you, or the judgment the
world will pass upon it."

She moved to the door, and passed through
it. Before the excited conversation into
which her guests fell could take definite form
or expression she returned, accompanied by
two ladies.

One was an elderly lady, whose bearing
was distinguished by a peculiar sadness and
dignity. The other was a lady, decently
dressed, upon whose face degradation had set

45*

its seal. Her cheeks were bloated, her eyes were bleared, her form trembled and shook, her hands were stretched forth helplessly, pitifully. Had it not been for the support of the elderly lady and Honoria, between whom she stood, the image of hopeless despair and imbecility, she would have fallen to the ground.

" This is my mother," said Honoria, drawing herself to her full height, " of whose existence I was aware only a few short weeks ago."

They gazed at her and her companions in silent wonder. For two or three minutes no word was spoken. Then Honoria turned to the elderly lady.

" Mrs. Kennedy," she said, " when my mother, then a young girl, was living in your home, she made the acquaintance of a man known to you and her as Mr. Julius Clifford. Kindly look around, and tell me if he is present in this toom."

" That is he," said Mrs. Kennedy, pointing to Mr. Haldane.

" Infamous! Infamous!"

The murmurs came from the guests. There was not one among them who could have claimed a spotless record, but they were not directly concerned in this adventure, and, being thus relieved, they were not slow in pronouncing judgment. The crime of the exposed man was that he had been found out; for such a crime there is no forgiveness; a man's own peers will unhesitatingly condemn him when he comes to this pass.

" Yes," said Honoria, " it is infamous. That man is my father, and for that man I entertain a horror too deep for utterance. This house, which once was his, belongs now to me. Who shall say that I, being his daughter, have no right here? Who shall say that my mother, who should have been his wife, has no right here? Let him carry away with him the memory of this scene as part of his punishment for his infamous crime. Human justice has failed, but by Divine judgment he stands condemned!"

She kissed her mother, and conducted her

and Mrs. Kennedy to the door. When those
two ladies were gone she spoke again :

" Mr. Haldane, you sleep not another night
under this roof, or under any roof which
covers me. You once turned another daughter, my half-sister, an angel of purity and
goodness, from your house, and threw her
upon the mercy of the world—as you threw
my mother upon its mercy. But her fate is a
happier one. I, who am not worthy to speak
her name, pray that God will shield and pro-
tect her, and make all her future bright and
happy! As you turned her from your house
I turn you now from mine. Mr. Redwood,
you and I have been for some time past playing a comedy—you called it so, I remember.
It is finished. The curtain has fallen. From
this night you and I are strangers. Gentlemen, farewell. I thank you for your patience.
Our acquaintance is at an end."

They bowed to her as she passed from the
room—all with the exception of Louis Redwood and Mr. Haldane. Louis Redwood
stood looking after her, chewing his mous-

tache ; there was a furious light in his eyes, but he knew that he was powerless, and that Honoria, the woman he had betrayed, had triumphed. Mr. Haldane, with his head bowed down, slunk away. Not a friendly word was spoken to him, not a friendly hand held out.

CHAPTER XLIV.

SISTERS.

Not more than a mile from Buckingham Palace Road stands a little church which still retains something of a rustic air, although it is within measurable distance of the heart of this great city, where the hum of restless, eager life is heard through all the waking hours of the day. An ancient tree has resisted the march of progress, and its branches spread over the pretty porch, birds' nests are there, which have witnessed many a happy mating, and when the snow is on the ground kind-hearted people throw crumbs to the sparrows who find shelter therein. A fitting place, therefore, for a wedding, in winter or summer—indeed, all the year round, for love has no special season, but buds and blossoms without reference to the calendar.

At the present time, which happens to be a sunny day in early October, a forgotten day in summer which has suddenly put in its claim, to the delight of old and young, there is a little gathering of idle people around the old church, basking in the sunshine, and listening to the twittering of the birds which this forgotten summer day is shamefully deceiving. Two weddings are to be celebrated there, and the idlers are waiting for the wedding parties. While they are chattering below on the roadway, and the birds are chattering above in the branches, with that special lightheartedness which distinguishes such occasions, a woman, plainly dressed and closely veiled, approaches the church, and enters it. No one takes any notice of her, the entire interest being absorbed in the wedding parties, the carriages containing which are just turning the corner of a street about thirty yards away. A murmur passes round. "Here they come—here they come," and the genially disposed idlers form themselves into two lines, with a sufficient space between to allow the important actors to pass through.

There are two carriages, which is rather a disappointment to the spectators, who would have preferred a dozen, or more ; but as in the arrangements for the weddings there was no reason why their inclinations should have been consulted they have no reasonable cause for complaint. They soon and quickly solace themselves by staring at the parties. From one of the carriages descend Agnes Haldane, Frederick Palmer, and his father, and Mr. Barlow. From the other Rachel Diprose, George Millington and his father, and Mrs. Barlow. Mr. Barlow is to give Miss Haldane away, and Mrs. Barlow stands female sponsor to Rachel Diprose.

There is a difference of opinion as to which of the brides is the prettier, but all are agreed that they are both the very picture of happiness. Perhaps for openly expressed happiness George Millington would take the palm, but joy is flowing in the hearts of brides and bridegrooms alike. Faithful love, tried in adversity, and never found wanting, is at length rewarded. The dark days are over, and though winter is near, love's sun is shining brightly and tenderly.

The words which bind each to the other are spoken. The rings are on the fingers, the kisses are exchanged, the names are signed. Agnes opens her arms to Rachel, and the girls are locked in a fond embrace.

"Dear Rachel!" murmurs Agnes, and can say no more, her heart is so full.

"My dear mistress!" murmurs Rachel.

What need for further words between them? Standing on the threshold of a new life these fair young creatures are the symbols of sweetness and faithfulness.

Rachel is the first to recover herself. She slips to the side of her George.

"You've got me at last, George," she says, crying and laughing at the same time.

"And I mean to keep you, Rachel," says George, kissing her again in the church—which I believe is against the regulations.

"But George, dear——"

" Yes, my darling ? "

" You were so impatient! I was almost afraid I was going to lose you, and that another girl would stand in my place."

" As if that could have ever happened!" says incredulous George. " Well, dad?"

" Well, my boy?" says Mr. Millington.

That is about all that passed between father and son. How feeble are written words! How eloquent are tones and looks!

Upon Agnes' finger is another plain ring of gold, with a single letter engraved upon its inner surface—H. Agnes looks around the church, and her eyes rest upon the figure of the woman still closely veiled, who had entered before the ceremony. She leaves her bridegroom's side, and goes to the pew in which this woman is standing.

" Honoria ! "

" Miss Haldane—forgive me—Mrs. Palmer !"

" Not to you, Honoria.   I am Agnes !"

" Agnes ! "

" Kiss me, sister ! "

" May you live a happy life !" murmured

Honoria. And the sisters embraced, and went their several ways. But before Honoria departed she called the clergyman and put a purse into his hand.

"Give this to poor people in your parish," she said, "from two happy brides."

THE END.

PRINTED BY

KELLY AND CO. LIMITED, GATE STREET, LINCOLN'S INN FIELDS, W.C.,

AND KINGSTON-ON-THAMES.

31, S,uthampton Street, Strand,
London, W.C.

F. V. WHITE & CO.'S

LIST OF

PUBLICATIONS.

NEW
NOVELS AT ALL CIRCULATING LIBRARIES.

NORA CREINA.
> By Mrs. HUNGERFORD, Author of "Molly Bawn," "April's Lady," &c. 3 vols.

THE MARCH OF FATE.
> By B. L. FARJEON, Author of "Great Porter Square," "Toilers of Babylon," &c. 3 vols.

WEDDED TO SPORT.
> By Mrs. EDWARD KENNARD, Author of "The Girl in the Brown Habit," "That Pretty Little Horsebreaker," &c. 3 vols.

MISS BLANCHARD OF CHICAGO.
> By ALBERT KEVILL DAVIES, Author of "Marriage up to Date," "An American Widow," &c. 3 vols.

FOR HIS SAKE.
> By Mrs. ALEXANDER, Author of "The Wooing O't," "Mona's Choice," &c. 3 vols.

A BIG STAKE.
> By Mrs. ROBERT JOCELYN, Author of "The M.F.H.'s Daughter," "The Criton Hunt Mystery," &c. 3 vols.

THE HON. JANE.
> By ANNIE THOMAS (Mrs. PENDER CUDLIP), Author of "Denis Donne," "Kate Valliant," &c. 3 vols.

WEAK WOMAN.
> By Mrs. LOVETT CAMERON, Author of "In a Grass Country," "Jack's Secret," &c. 3 vols.

THE NOBLER SEX.
> By FLORENCE MARRYAT, Author of "My Sister the Actress," &c. 3 vols.

A MODERN BRIDEGROOM.
> By Mrs. ALEXANDER FRASER, Author of "Daughters of Belgravia," &c. 2 vols.

ETERNAL ENMITY.
> By FRANCIS FRANCIS, Author of "Saddle and Mocassin," &c. 2 vols. 12s.

OLD DACRES' DARLING.
> By ANNIE THOMAS (Mrs. Pender Cudlip), Author of "Denis Donne," "The Honble. Jane," &c. 3 vols.

EDLEEN VAUGHAN; OR, PATHS OF PERIL.
> By "CARMEN SYLVA" (Her Majesty the Queen of Roumania). 3 vols.

F. V. WHITE & CO., 31, Southampton Street, Strand.

THE WORKS OF JOHN STRANGE WINTER.

UNIFORM IN STYLE AND PRICE.

Each in Paper Covers, 1/-; Cloth, 1/6.   (At all Booksellers' &
Bookstalls.)

WINTER'S CHRISTMAS ANNUAL. (8th Year
of Publication.) THOSE GIRLS.

MERE LUCK.   (3rd Edition.)

LUMLEY THE PAINTER.   (3rd Edition.)

GOOD-BYE.   (6th Edition.)

HE WENT FOR A SOLDIER.   (7th Edition.)

FERRERS COURT.   (5th Edition.)

BUTTONS.   (7th Edition.)

A LITTLE FOOL.   (9th Edition.)

MY POOR DICK.

(9th Edition.) Illustrated by MAURICE GREIFFENHAGEN.

BOOTLES' CHILDREN.

(10th Edition.) Illustrated by J. BERNARD PARTRIDGE.

"John Strange Winter is never more thoroughly at home than when delineating
the characters of children, and everyone will be delighted with the dignified Madge
and the quaint Pearl. The book is mainly occupied with the love affairs of Terry
(the soldier servant who appears in many of the preceding books), but the children
buzz in and out of its pages much as they would come in and out of a room in real
life, pervading and brightening the house in which they dwell."—*Leicester Daily
Post.*

THE CONFESSIONS OF A PUBLISHER.

"The much discussed question of the relations between a publisher and his clients
furnishes Mr. John Strange Winter with material for one of the brightest tales of
the season. Abel Drinkwater's autobiography is written from a humorous point of
view; yet here, as elsewhere, 'many a true word is spoken in jest,' and in the con-
versations of the publisher and his too ingenuous son facts come to light that are
worthy of the attention of aspirants to literary fame."—*Morning Post.*

MIGNON'S HUSBAND.   (13th Edition.)

"It is a capital love story, full of high spirits, and written in a dashing style that
will charm the most melancholy of readers into hearty enjoyment of its fun."—
Scotsman.

THAT IMP.   (11th Edition.)

"Barrack life is abandoned for the nonce, and the author of 'Bootles' Baby'
introduces readers to a country home replete with every comfort, and containing
men and women whose acquaintanceship we can only regret can never blossom into
friendship.'—*Whitehall Review.*

"This charming little book is bright and breezy, and has the ring of supreme
truth about it."—*Vanity Fair.*

MIGNON'S SECRET.   (16th Edition.)

"In 'Mignon's Secret' Mr. Winter has supplied a continuation to the never-to-
be-forgotten 'Bootles' Baby.' . . . The story is gracefully and touchingly
told."—*John Bull.*

F. V. WHITE & Co., 31, Southampton Street, Strand.

THE WORKS OF JOHN STRANGE WINTER—*(continued).*

ON MARCH.   (9th Edition.)

"This short story is characterised by Mr. Winter's customary truth in detail, humour, and pathos."—*Academy.*

" By publishing ' On March,' Mr J. S. Winter has added another little gem to his well-known store of regimental sketches. The story is written with humour and a deal of feeling."—*Army & Navy Gazette.*

IN QUARTERS.   (11th Edition.)

"' In Quarters' is one of those rattling tales of soldiers' life which the public have learned to thoroughly appreciate."—*The Graphic.*

" The author of ' Bootles' Baby ' gives us here another story of military life, which few have better described."—*British Quarterly Review.*

ARMY SOCIETY ; Life in a Garrison Town.

Cloth, 6/-; also in Picture Boards, 2/-. (10th Edition.)

"This discursive story, dealing with life in a garrison town, is full of pleasant ' go ' and movement which has distinguished ' Bootles' Baby,' ' Pluck,' or in fact a majority of some half-dozen novelettes which the author has submitted to the eyes of railway bookstall patronisers."—*Daily Telegraph.*

" The strength of the book lies in its sketches of life in a garrison town, which are undeniably clever. . . . It is pretty clear that Mr. Winter draws from life."—*St. James's Gazette.*

GARRISON GOSSIP, Gathered in Blankhampton.

(A Sequel to "ARMY SOCIETY,") Cloth, 2/6; also in Picture Boards, 2/- (5th Edition.)

"' Garrison Gossip' may fairly rank with ' Cavalry Life,' and the various other books with which Mr. Winter has so agreeably beguiled our leisure hours."—*Saturday Review.*

" The novel fully maintains the reputation which its author has been fortunate enough to gain in a special line of his own."—*Graphic.*

A SIEGE BABY.   Cloth, 2/6 ; Picture boards, 2/- (4th Edition.)

"The story which gives its title to this new sheaf of stories by the popular author of ' Bootles' Baby ' is a very touching and pathetic one. . . . Amongst the other stories, the one entitled, ' Out of the Mists' is, perhaps, the best written, although the tale of true love it embodies comes to a most melancholy ending."—*County Gentlemen.*

BEAUTIFUL JIM.   (8th Edition.)

Cloth Gilt, 2/6 ; also Picture Boards, 2/-

MRS. BOB.   (6th Edition.)

Cloth gilt, 2/6. Also Picture Boards, 2/-

THE OTHER MAN'S WIFE.   (4th Edition.)

Cloth, 2/6.

MY GEOFF ; or, The Experiences of a Lady-Help.   (A New Novel.) (3rd Edition.) Cloth, 2/6.

MRS. EDWARD KENNARD'S SPORTING NOVELS.

(At all Booksellers' and Bookstalls.)

THAT PRETTY LITTLE HORSE-BREAKER.
Cloth gilt, 2s. 6d.   (3rd Edition.)

A HOMBURG BEAUTY.   (3rd Edition.)   Cloth gilt, 2s. 6d.
Picture Boards, 2s.

MATRON OR MAID?   (4th Edition.)
Cloth gilt, 2s. 6d. ; Picture Boards, 2s.

LANDING A PRIZE.   (6th Edition.)
Cloth gilt, 2s. 6d. Picture Boards, 2/-

A CRACK COUNTY.   (6th Edition.)
Cloth gilt, 2/6 ; Picture Boards, 2s.

THE GIRL IN THE BROWN HABIT.
Cloth gilt, 2/6 ; Picture Boards, 2/-.   (7th Edition.)

"'Nell Fitzgerald' is an irreproachable heroine, full of gentle womanliness, and rich in all virtues that make her kind estimable. Mrs. Kennard's work is marked by high tone as well as vigorous narrative, and sportsmen, when searching for something new and beguiling for a wet day or spell of frost, can hardly light upon anything better than these fresh and picturesque hunting stories of Mrs. Kennard's."— *Daily Telegraph.*

KILLED IN THE OPEN.
Cloth gilt, 2/6 ; Picture Boards, 2/-.   (8th Edition.)

"It is in truth a very good love story set in a framework of hounds and horses, but one that could be read with pleasure independently of any such attractions."— *Fortnightly Review.*
"'Killed in the Open' is a very superior sort of hunting novel indeed."— *Graphic.*

STRAIGHT AS A DIE.
Cloth gilt, 2/6 ; Picture Boards, 2/-.   (8th Edition.)

"If you like sporting novels I can recommend to you Mrs. Kennard's 'Straight as a Die.'"—*Truth.*

A REAL GOOD THING.
Cloth gilt, 2/6 ; Picture Boards, 2/-.   (7th Edition.)

"There are some good country scenes and country spins in 'A Real Good Thing.' The hero, poor old Hopkins, is a strong character."—*Academy.*

OUR FRIENDS IN THE HUNTING-FIELD.
Cloth gilt, 2s. 6d. ; Picture Boards, 2s.

BY THE SAME AUTHOR.
In Paper Covers, 1/-; Cloth, 1/6.

THE MYSTERY OF A WOMAN'S HEART.

HAWLEY SMART'S SPORTING NOVELS.

(At all Booksellers' and Bookstalls.)

BEATRICE AND BENEDICK: A Romance of the Crimea.   Cloth, 2 6.

THE PLUNGER.   Cloth gilt, 2 6. Picture Boards, 2/-. (4th Edition.)

LONG ODDS.   Cloth gilt, 2,6. Picture Boards, 2/- (5th Edition.)

THE MASTER OF RATHKELLY.
Cloth gilt, 2/6. Picture Boards, 2/- (5th Edition.)

THE OUTSIDER.   Cloth gilt, 2/6. Picture Boards, 2/- (7th Edition.)

BY THE SAME AUTHOR. Each in Paper Covers. 1/-;   Cloth, 1/6.

A MEMBER OF TATTERSALL'S.

A BLACK BUSINESS.   (3rd Edition.)

THRICE PAST THE POST.   (3rd Edition.)

NOVELS
By B. L. FARJEON.

(At all Booksellers' and Bookstalls.)
In Cloth, 2/6.

BASIL AND ANNETTE.

THE MYSTERY OF M. FELIX.

A YOUNG GIRL'S LIFE.
(3rd Edition.) Also Picture Boards, 2 -

TOILERS OF BABYLON.   Also Picture Boards, 2/-

THE DUCHESS OF ROSEMARY LANE.

In Paper Covers, 1 -; Cloth, 1,6.

A VERY YOUNG COUPLE.

THE PERIL OF RICHARD PARDON. (2nd Edition.)

A STRANGE ENCHANTMENT.
By the Author of "Devlin the Barber." &c.

BY THE HONOURABLE MRS. FETHERSTONHAUGH.
(At all Booksellers' and Bookstalls.)

DREAM FACES.   By the Author of "Kilcorran," "Robin Adair," &c. Cloth, 2/6.

BY BRET HARTE.
(At all Booksellers' and Bookstalls.)

THE CRUSADE OF THE "EXCELSIOR."
By the Author of "The Luck of Roaring Camp," &c. Cloth, 2/6; Picture Boards, 2/-.

SIR RANDAL ROBERTS' SPORTING NOVEL.
(At all Booksellers' and Bookstalls.)

CURB AND SNAFFLE.   By the Author of "In the Shires," &c. Cloth gilt. 2/6

BY MRS. ALEXANDER FRASER.
(At all Booksellers' and Bookstalls.)

THE NEW DUCHESS. (2nd Edition.) Cloth, 2s. 6d.

DAUGHTERS OF BELGRAVIA   Cloth, 2/6. Also Picture Boards, 2 -

SHE CAME BETWEEN.   Cloth, 2 6.

MRS. LOVETT CAMERON'S NOVELS.
(At all Booksellers' and Bookstalls.)

IN A GRASS COUNTRY.
(A Story of Love and Sport.) (9th Edition.) Paper Covers 1/-.

"We turn with pleasure to the green covers of 'In a Grass Country.' The three heroines are charming each in her own way. It is well sketched, full of character, with sharp observations of men and women—not too hard on anybody—a clear story carefully written, and therefore easily read. . . . recommended." *Punch.*

"When the days are short and there is an hour or two to be disposed of indoors before dressing time, one is glad to be able to recommend a good and amusing novel. 'In a Grass Country' may be said to come under this description."—*Saturday Review.*

JACK'S SECRET.   Cloth, 2 6.

A LOST WIFE (3rd Edition.) Cloth, 2/6. Picture Boards, 2 -

A DAUGHTER'S HEART.   Cloth, 2s. 6d.

TWO NOVELS by
JUSTIN M'CARTHY, M.P.
AND
MRS. CAMPBELL PRAED.
(Authors of "The Right Honourable," &c.)
Cloth, 2s. 6d. each; also in Picture Boards, 2s.
(At all Booksellers' and Bookstalls.)

THE LADIES' GALLERY. (2nd Edition.)

THE RIVAL PRINCESS; a London Romance of To-day.
(3rd Edition.)

MRS. ALEXANDER'S NOVELS.

(At all Booksellers' and Bookstalls.)

A WOMAN'S HEART.   Cloth, 2.6

BLIND FATE.   Cloth, 2.6.   Picture Boards, 2 -

WELL WON.   (2nd. Edition.) Paper Covers, 1/-; Cloth, 1/6.

BY WOMAN'S WIT   (6th Edition.) Picture Boards, 2/-. Cloth, 2 6

> "In Mrs. Alexander's tale
> Much art she clearly shows
> In keeping dark the mystery
> Until the story's close!"—*Punch*.

MONA'S CHOICE.   (5th Edition.) Cloth, 2/6.   Picture Boards 2'

NOVELS BY HUME NISBET.

(At all Booksellers' and Bookstalls.)

THE BUSHRANGER'S SWEETHEART; AN AUSTRALIAN ROMANCE.   With original Illustrations by the Author. Cloth, 3.6. (3rd Edition.)

THE SAVAGE QUEEN; A ROMANCE OF THE NATIVES OF VAN DIEMAN'S LAND.
Cloth, 2s. 6d.; Picture Boards, 2s. (3rd Edition.)

"RITA'S" NOVELS.

(AT ALL BOOKSELLERS' AND BOOKSTALLS.

THE LAIRD O' COCKPEN.   Cloth, 2/6.

SHEBA; A STUDY OF GIRLHOOD.
(3rd Edition.) Cloth, 2.6. Picture Boards, 2:-

MISS KATE.   (4th Edition.) Cloth, 2 6; Picture Boards, 2/0.

THE SEVENTH DREAM.   1.- and 1.6.

THE DOCTOR'S SECRET.   (2nd Edition.) 1.- and 1/6.

AMYE READE'S NEW WORK.

(At all Booksellers' and Bookstalls.)

SLAVES OF THE SAWDUST.   By the Author of "Ruby," &c.
Picture Boards, 2/-. Also Cloth, 2 6.

(Dedicated, by permission, to Lord Tennyson.)

POPULAR WORKS

By WILLIAM DAY,

(Author of " The Racehorse in Training," " Reminiscences of the Turf," &c.)

TURF CELEBRITIES I HAVE KNOWN.

With a Portrait of the Author.

1 Vol. 16s.

(At all Libraries and Booksellers.)

By GUSTAV FREYTAG.

REMINISCENCES OF MY LIFE.

Translated from the German by KATHARINE CHETWYND.

In Two Vols. 18s.

(At all Libraries and Booksellers.)

By MRS. ARMSTRONG,

(Author of " Modern Etiquette in Public and Private.")

GOOD FORM.

A BOOK OF EVERY DAY ETIQUETTE.

(2nd Edition.) Limp Cloth, 2s.

(At all Booksellers' and Bookstalls.)

By PERCY THORPE.

HISTORY OF JAPAN.

Cloth, 3s. 6d.

(At all Booksellers' and Bookstalls.)

By PARNELL GREENE.

ON THE BANKS OF THE DEE.

A LEGEND OF CHESTER.

Cloth, 5s.

(At all Booksellers' and Bookstalls.)

By W. GERARD.

BYRON RE-STUDIED IN HIS DRAMAS.

Cloth, 5s.

THE VISION, AND OTHER POEMS.

Cloth, 3s. 6d.

(At all Booksellers' and Bookstalls.)

F. V. WHITE & CO., 31, Southampton Street, Strand.

ONE VOLUME NOVELS
BY POPULAR AUTHORS.

Crown 8vo., Cloth, 2s. 6d. each.

(AT ALL BOOKSELLERS' AND BOOKSTALLS.)

By JOHN STRANGE WINTER.

MY GEOFF.	BEAUTIFUL JIM.
THE OTHER MAN'S WIFE.	A SIEGE BABY.
MRS. BOB.	GARRISON GOSSIP.

By MRS. EDWARD KENNARD.

THAT PRETTY LITTLE HORSE-BREAKER.
A HOMBURG BEAUTY.
MATRON OR MAID?
LANDING A PRIZE.
A CRACK COUNTY.
A REAL GOOD THING.
STRAIGHT AS A DIE.
THE GIRL IN THE BROWN HABIT.
KILLED IN THE OPEN.
OUR FRIENDS IN THE HUNTING-FIELD.

By HAWLEY SMART.

BEATRICE AND BENEDICK.
THE PLUNGER.
LONG ODDS.
THE MASTER OF RATHKELLY.
THE OUTSIDER.

By MRS. CAMPBELL PRAED.

THE ROMANCE OF A CHALET.

By B. L. FARJEON.

BASIL AND ANNETTE.
THE MYSTERY OF M. FELIX.
A YOUNG GIRL'S LIFE.
TOILERS OF BABYLON.
THE DUCHESS OF ROSEMARY LANE.

By MAY CROMMELIN.

THE FREAKS OF LADY FORTUNE.

By FLORENCE WARDEN.

A WITCH OF THE HILLS.
A WILFUL WARD.

By MABEL COLLINS.

VIOLA FANSHAWE.

By B. M. CROKER.

TWO MASTERS.	INTERFERENCE.

By HUME NISBET.

THE SAVAGE QUEEN.

F. V. WHITE & CO., 31, Southampton Street, Strand.

ONE VOLUME NOVELS—*(continued)*.

By AMYE READE, Author of "RUBY," &c.
SLAVES OF THE SAWDUST.

By F. C. PHILIPS & C. J. WILLS.
SYBIL ROSS'S MARRIAGE.

By MRS. ALEXANDER.

BLIND FATE.	MONA'S CHOICE.
BY WOMAN'S WIT.	A WOMAN'S HEART

By MRS. LOVETT CAMERON.

JACK'S SECRET.	A DAUGHTER'S HEART.
A LOST WIFE.	

By JUSTIN M'CARTHY, M.P. & Mrs. CAMPBELL PRAED.
THE LADIES' GALLERY.
THE RIVAL PRINCESS.

By MRS. ROBERT JOCELYN.

THE M.F.H.'s DAUGHTER.	DRAWN BLANK.
THE CRITON HUNT MYSTERY.	

By BRET HARTE.
THE CRUSADE OF THE "EXCELSIOR."

By the Honble. MRS. FETHERSTONHAUGH
DREAM FACES.

By FERGUS HUME.
WHOM GOD HATH JOINED.
THE MAN WITH A SECRET.
MISS MEPHISTOPHELES.

By Mrs. HUNGERFORD, (Author of "MOLLY BAWN.")
THE HONBLE. MRS. VEREKER.
A LIFE'S REMORSE.
APRIL'S LADY.
LADY PATTY.

By "RITA."
SHEBA.
MISS KATE.
THE LAIRD O' COCKPEN.

By MRS. ALEXANDER FRASER.
THE NEW DUCHESS.
DAUGHTERS OF BELGRAVIA.
SHE CAME BETWEEN.

By MAY CROMMELIN and J. MORAY BROWN.
VIOLET VYVIAN, M.F.H.

By F. C. PHILIPS and PERCY FENDALL.
A DAUGHTER'S SACRIFICE.
MARGARET BYNG.
MY FACE IS MY FORTUNE.

" POPULAR " NOVELS.

Picture Boards, 2s. each.

(AT ALL BOOKSELLERS' AND BOOKSTALLS.)

MRS. BOB. (6th Edition.) By JOHN STRANGE WINTER.

BEAUTIFUL JIM. (8th Edition.) By same Author.

A SIEGE BABY. (4th Edition.) By same Author.

GARRISON GOSSIP. (5th Edition.) By same Author.

ARMY SOCIETY: Life in a Garrison Town. (10th Edition.) By the same Author.

MISS MEPHISTOPHELES. (5th Edition.) By FERGUS HUME.

THE MAN WITH A SECRET. (4th Edition.) By the same Author.

LONG ODDS. (5th Edition.) By HAWLEY SMART.

THE PLUNGER. (4th Edition.) By the same Author.

THE MASTER OF RATHKELLY. (5th Edition.) By the same Author.

THE OUTSIDER. (7th Edition.) By the same Author.

A LOST WIFE. (3rd Edition.) By Mrs. LOVETT CAMERON.

MONA'S CHOICE. (5th Edition.) By Mrs. ALEXANDER.

BLIND FATE. By the same Author.

BY WOMAN'S WIT. (6th Edition.) By the same Author.

THE HON. MRS. VEREKER. By Mrs. HUNGERFORD, Author of "Molly Bawn."

A LIFE'S REMORSE. (3rd Edition.) By the same Author.

LANDING A PRIZE. (6th Edition.) By Mrs. EDWARD KENNARD.

A HOMBURG BEAUTY. (3rd Edition.) By the same Author.

MATRON OR MAID? (4th Edition.) By the same Author.

A CRACK COUNTY. (6th Edition.) By the same Author.

A REAL GOOD THING. (7th Edition.) By the same Author.

STRAIGHT AS A DIE. (8th Edition.) By the same Author.

THE GIRL IN THE BROWN HABIT. (7th Edition.) By the same Author.

OUR FRIENDS IN THE HUNTING-FIELD. By the same Author.

F. V. WHITE & CO., 31, Southampton Street, Strand.

"POPULAR" NOVELS—*(continued).*

KILLED IN THE OPEN. (8th Edition.) By the same Author.

SHEBA; A Study of Girlhood. (3rd Edition.) By "RITA."

MISS KATE; or, Confessions of a Caretaker. (4th Edition.) By the same Author.

TOILERS OF BABYLON. By B. L FARJEON.

A YOUNG GIRL'S LIFE. (3rd Edition.) By the same Author.

THE RIVAL PRINCESS. (3rd Edition.) By JUSTIN McCARTHY, M.P., and Mrs. CAMPBELL PRAED.

THE LADIES' GALLERY. (2nd Edition.) By the same Authors.

A WOMAN'S FACE. By FLORENCE WARDEN, Author of "The House on the Marsh," &c.

VIOLET VYVIAN, M.F.H. (2nd Edition.) By MAY CROMMELIN and J. MORAY BROWN.

DAUGHTERS OF BELGRAVIA. By Mrs. ALEXANDER FRASER.

SYBIL ROSS'S MARRIAGE: The Romance of an Inexperienced Girl. (3rd Edition.) By F. C. PHILIPS and C. J. WILLS.

A DAUGHTER'S SACRIFICE. By F. C. PHILIPS and PERCY FENDALL.

THE HEART OF JANE WARNER. By FLORENCE MARRYAT.

UNDER THE LILIES AND ROSES. By the same Author.

KATE VALLIANT. By ANNIE THOMAS (Mrs. PENDER CUDLIP).

MATED WITH A CLOWN. By LADY CONSTANCE HOWARD.

KEITH'S WIFE. By LADY VIOLET GREVILLE.

THE CRUSADE OF THE "EXCELSIOR." By BRET HARTE.

SLAVES OF THE SAWDUST. (A New and Original Work.) By AMYE READE, Author of "Ruby," &c. (Dedicated, by permission, to Lord Tennyson.) Also in cloth, 2 6.

NOT EASILY JEALOUS. By IZA DUFFUS HARDY.

ONLY A LOVE STORY. By the same Author.

POISONED ARROWS. By JEAN MIDDLEMASS.

THE SAVAGE QUEEN: A Romance of the Natives of Van Dieman's Land. (3rd Edition.) By HUME NISBET.

THE M.F.H.'s DAUGHTER. By Mrs. ROBERT JOCELYN.

ONE SHILLING NOVELS.

In Paper Covers. (Cloth, 1s. 6d.)

(At all Booksellers' and Bookstalls.)

WINTER'S CHRISTMAS ANNUAL. (8th Year of Publication.) THOSE GIRLS. By JOHN STRANGE WINTER, Author of "Bootles' Baby," &c.

MERE LUCK. (3rd Edition.) By the same Author.

LUMLEY THE PAINTER. (3rd Edition.) By the same Author.

GOOD-BYE. (6th Edition.) By the same Author.

HE WENT FOR A SOLDIER. (7th Edition.) By the same Author.

FERRERS COURT. (5th Edition.) By the same Author.

BUTTONS. (7th Edition.) By the same Author.

A LITTLE FOOL. (9th Edition.) By the same Author.

MY POOR DICK. (Illustrated by MAURICE GREIFFEN-HAGEN.) (9th Edition.) By the same Author.

BOOTLES' CHILDREN. (Illustrated by J. BERNARD PARTRIDGE.) (10th Edition.) By the same Author.

THE CONFESSIONS OF A PUBLISHER. By the same Author.

MIGNON'S HUSBAND. (13th Edition.) By the same Author.

THAT IMP. (11th Edition.) By the same Author.

MIGNON'S SECRET. (16th Edition.) By the same Author.

ON MARCH. (9th Edition.) By the same Author.

IN QUARTERS. (11th Edition.) By the same Author.

THE GENTLEMAN WHO VANISHED. (2nd Edition.) By FERGUS HUME.

THE PICCADILLY PUZZLE. By the same Author.

THE POWER OF AN EYE. By Mrs. FRANK ST. CLAIR GRIMWOOD, Author of "My Three Years in Manipur."

A VERY YOUNG COUPLE. By B. L. FARJEON, Author of "Toilers of Babylon," &c.

THE PERIL OF RICHARD PARDON. (2nd Edition.) By the same Author.

A STRANGE ENCHANTMENT. By the same Author.

F. V. WHITE & Co., 31, Southampton Street, Strand.

ONE SHILLING NOVELS—*(continued)*.

THE MYSTERY OF No. 13. (2nd Edition.) By HELEN MATHERS, Author of "Comin' Thro' the Rye," &c.

MY JO, JOHN. By HELEN MATHERS. (2nd Edition.)

T'OTHER DEAR CHARMER. By the same Author.

WELL WON. By Mrs. ALEXANDER, Author of "The Wooing O't," "Blind Fate," &c. (2nd Edition.)

TOM'S WIFE. By Lady MARGARET MAJENDIE, Author of "Fascination," "Sisters-in-Law," &c.

THE CONFESSIONS OF A DOOR MAT. By ALFRED C. CALMOUR. Author of "The Amber Heart," &c.

THE MYSTERY OF A WOMAN'S HEART. By Mrs. EDWARD KENNARD.

IN A GRASS COUNTRY. By Mrs. LOVETT CAMERON. (9th Edition.)

CITY AND SUBURBAN. (2nd Edition.) By FLORENCE WARDEN, Author of "The House on the Marsh," &c.

A SHOCK TO SOCIETY. (3rd Edition.) By the same Author.

THE DOCTOR'S SECRET. (2nd Edition.) By "RITA," Author of "Dame Durden," "Sheba," &c.

THE SEVENTH DREAM. By the same Author.

A BLACK BUSINESS. (3rd Edition.) By HAWLEY SMART, Author of "The Outsider," &c.

A MEMBER OF TATTERSALL'S. By the same Author.

THRICE PAST THE POST. (3rd Edition.) By the same Author.

HER LAST THROW. (2nd Edition.) By Mrs. HUNGERFORD, Author of "Molly Bawn," &c.

A CONQUERING HEROINE. By the same Author.

TWO ON AN ISLAND. By CURTIS YORKE, Author of "Hush!" "A Romance of Modern London," &c.

THE MYSTERY OF BELGRAVE SQUARE. By the same Author. (In cloth, only.)

A FRENCH MARRIAGE. By F. C. PHILIPS.

FACING THE FOOTLIGHTS. By FLORENCE MARRYAT.

www.ingramcontent.com/pod-product-compliance
Lightning Source LLC
Chambersburg PA
CBHW020356030726
47496CB00007B/2172